It is a decision in the penalty area of a floodlit football field that sets off the events leading to a horrific murder.

The football hooligans who wreck trains, fight, throw lavatory rolls and commit other acts of mindless 'aggro' in support of their teams are a current social phenomenon. One such gang – its leadership, its composition, its girls, its attitudes – is here shown in all its dreadful detail. This gang goes as far as murder.

The subsequent police investigation is detailed, meticulous – and partially successful. The judicial processes that follow, including scenes from the trial, themselves provide an ironical comment on the various destinies of evil persons.

This is an exciting, authentic story, very much of our own times. The author of *Swansong for a Rare Bird* (one of the runners-up in the Macmillan/Panther first crime novel competition) has successfully defied the bogey of a second novel with this gripping narrative.

By the same author

Swansong for a Rare Bird

ALFRED DRAPER

The Death Penalty

MACMILLAN

SBN Boards: 333 13352 8

First published 1972 by
MACMILLAN LONDON LTD
London and Basingstoke
Associated companies in New York Toronto
Dublin Melbourne Johannesburg & Madras

Printed in Great Britain by
RICHARD CLAY (THE CHAUCER PRESS LTD
Bungay, Suffolk

Henry Clegg sat in his armchair dabbing the tip of his tongue with the stub of an indelible pencil, his forehead creased in concentration, the copy coupon of his pools entry balanced on his right knee. Five feet away the television screen was rolling the football results, while an emotionless voice repeated the scores. Over the years he had managed to develop a technique of anticipating the scores by the merest change of inflection in the announcer's voice.

Clegg put his carpet-slippered foot under the belly of his mongrel bitch who was scratching an ear with a hind leg, and hoisted her away from the fire. Not that she was distracting him – it was merely a gesture of annoyance that one of his bankers had let him down. The mongrel yelped more in protest than pain, and began to nudge her master's knee with her nostril. Henry tickled the top of her head with his free hand to indicate there was nothing personal in the assault.

He cursed from time to time as yet another result failed to conform to his forecast, but the cussing was no reflection of a sportsman's disappointment, for he had no real interest in the game as such. It was years since he had stood shivering on the terraces watching two teams trying to stop each other from scoring. Leastways, that was how Henry saw football in, 'This modern day and age'. In the local he always complained about the present day negative approach by players, and this was a cue for him to hark back to the good old days, 'When football meant scoring bloody goals, not this modern crap of stopping the others at all costs. It's

5

all bloody negative. Negative.'

But if Henry had told the truth he would have confessed that football to him was nothing more than a list of fixtures which offered the chance of paradise. Heaven on earth. During the Saturday ritual of checking results his mind was always neatly divided: one half was absorbed with the quest for those elusive draws which would make him a rich man overnight, and end for ever the soul-destroying drudgery of loading slop bins in the hotel where he worked as a kitchen porter. The other half of his mind had already achieved the goal. He lay on an egg-timer sand beach, salt-sized grains trickling through his fingers, watching Cambridge-blue waves smack into a coral reef sending up spumes of detergent-white spray, while a sarong-clad girl handed him ice-chilled drinks and propositioned him with dark lustful eyes. And his loutish son Ben wouldn't even get a look in. The bastard. All he was fit for was putting the boot in and butting some poor unfortunate sod.

At one stage, not too long ago either, he would have put him well and truly in his place with a bloody good clout round the ear. But Little Ben now towered above him, and he secretly feared he would get a wallop back. Now he always felt a sense of inadequacy in his presence. Even if he could find the words, he doubted if he could get through to his son. He was frustratingly unable to understand him, or what he wanted out of life. All he knew was that Ben lived and loved every minute of life, and was content with his lot, and that he could not understand.

' 'En, you'll just have to get some new shirts. I've patched and darned this one so much there's no tail to it.' The voice was tired and not really anticipating a reply.

Henry looked towards his wife who was working under the centre light in the room, testing the iron from time to time by spitting on the base or holding it against her cheek.

6

'Jesus, woman. How many times have I told you not to bloody interrupt when I'm checking my coupon? It would be real charming if I ballsed up the coupon because you were nattering.'

The harsh rebuke was unnecessary, for Henry had conceded that his hopes of a life of luxury would have to be deferred until next week, but it made him feel that it was his wife's fault that once again the Eldorado of unlimited wealth had eluded him. Bitterness flooded through him because he knew from the announcer's cheerful remarks that the dividend would be a big one, and later in the week the newspapers would show some goggle-eyed git being handed a cheque by a sexy film star.

'Don't get so down in the dumps, 'En. Our turn will come, just you see.'

'I hope so, May. I really do. What narks me most is that some silly mug will win it who don't know what to do with it.'

'Blimey, 'En, wouldn't we show them if we just had the luck!' She stopped ironing to luxuriate in the prospect of what it would all mean. 'I bet we'd find a lot of friends we never knew we had.' The thought encouraged her to add zest to her final bit of ironing.

Henry rolled himself a match-stick-thick cigarette with adept fingers and nodded. He deliberately refrained from commenting on his wife's remark, because when that golden day did come there was no danger of a crowd of hangers on. No one would even know when the golden apple fell, for one cross went on to his coupon religiously each week indicating that the sender had no wish for publicity; and by the time it leaked out, they would be far away, uncontactable and untouchable on his dream beach.

Henry rose from his chair, devoured by a sense of emptiness, now that the one moment in the week he longed for had ended again so disappointingly.

'Seen the dog's collar?'

The planing movement of the iron stopped. 'You going out then?'

'Thought I'd just give the pooch a stretch and get myself a classified.'

'What for? You know the results. Anyway, you never read the paper. It lies around unopened till Little Ben comes home. Anyway, if you can wait five more minutes I'll have finished and walk down with you.'

'You know you don't like it down there with us men just nattering at the bar.'

'Others take their wives. You ashamed of me?'

'No. If you want to come O.K. But hurry up. And another thing, stop calling him Little Ben; it makes me want to throw up. He's as big as a guardsman now, and twice as bloody ugly.'

May said, 'Oh, all right.' But he knew it would make no difference. She would soon relapse into the habit of calling their hulk of a son by his nickname. A nickname that had persisted since he was a small boy, and been taken on a summer morning's outing to Westminster where he had stood on the bridge by Boadicea's statue and looked upwards at the clock as its chimes boomed out. When he had been told the name, he had delighted his parents by pointing to himself and saying, 'I'm Little Ben.' The name had stuck with his mother, although the joke had years ago worn thin for his father.

The Cleggs' council flat was on the fifth floor of a new multi-storey block. But London's smog, grit and exhaust fumes were gradually turning them into an architect-designed slum.

The front door-bell rang. Mrs Clegg said, 'He must have forgotten his key again.'

8

'He'd lose his head if it wasn't screwed on,' said Henry, the loathing evident in his voice.

The lid of the letter-box was lifted and Ben shouted through, 'Come on, open up. It's parky out here.'

Henry made no attempt to go towards the door, and his wife said sarcastically, 'Stay there, I'll go.'

Henry's deep obsessional loathing for his only child was not born out of any sense of disappointment at what he had sired, but, as he secretly admitted, sheer envy. Ben was everything he would have liked to be himself. Self-assured to the point of cockiness, content with his well paid dead-end job of washing down other people's cars without any covetous envy, his horizon bounded only by the fortunes of the football team whose pylon-mounted floodlights could be seen from the roof of the flats. Ben was not awed as he was by authority, or petrified by a policeman's voice. In fact, he referred to them contemptuously as the 'Fuzz' or 'Mr Plod'.

Ben's bedroom was a museum-cum-shrine to his team. The walls were covered with coloured pictures of the players – front row seated, rear row standing, arms folded in laundry-fresh strip with the trainer at one end, manager at the other. There were cut-out action pictures of his idols kicking, heading, trapping or throwing a ball. Triangular pennants recording overseas visits hung by their silk cords, on a bedside table lay a thick book full of press cuttings chronicling the team's achievements. And neatly stacked in date order were the programmes of matches played both at home and away.

Ben lived for his team and there was no more loyal supporter. When they won it was justly deserved, when they lost they were 'robbed', and anyone who disagreed could 'come outside'. No palm-beaches beckoned him, his globe was a football, his Mecca Wembley Stadium with his team's

9

skipper holding aloft the F.A. cup.

When the season ended he spent the summer roaring around the country on his moped seeking the distraction of some 'aggro', and passing the time away with acts of vandalism. His natural enemies were hippies who wore beads and dangled flowers. Homosexuals were not subjects for compassion but targets for a little diverting 'queer bashing'.

When Ben came into the room, he slackened and tightened a six-foot long red-and-orange-striped scarf above his head, and performed the steps of a primitive victory dance before flopping heavily into an armchair.

'All right, so you won. But you don't have to knock a hole in the floor. I heard the score on telly,' said his father.

Tall, thick-shouldered, Ben's face bore a petulant expression as if he knew trouble was never far away. His sandy hair was cut so short it was little longer than the stubble of a week old beard. He wore a tie-less button-down-collar shirt of thick grey flannel, a pair of Micawber-short trousers held up by braces of slim webbing, and a pair of cherry red 'bovver' boots, with soles as thick-ridged as heavy duty car tyres, and toe caps which were reinforced by a steel-hard plastic.

His repetitive phrases angered his father as he began to recount the game:

'Look, man, dead seriously. We hammered them. Honest. We should have been six up at half time, not two, but for that stinking square ref. He hid behind a bloody escort of fuzz he was so shit scared what would happen if the fans got hold of him.' And in the same breath, 'Any grub, Mum?'

Henry made it sound as if he was being forced out of his own home. 'I'm going down for my paper. I can't bear to hear a lad using that kind of language in his own house. Come on, Meg.'

The dog slunk up to him and cringed as the lead was clipped on to her collar, dreading the weekly torture of lying in a bar with the lead trapped below the leg of a bar stool, while enormous legs hemmed her in and big shoes trod on her paws.

'Do leave Ben alone. No sooner is he in the house than you're getting on at him. I don't know why you moan about him having a lovely outdoor interest,' said his mother. Then petulantly, 'Aren't you waiting for me?'

'I thought you was getting his food. I'll see you down there.'

When he had gone, Ben occupied the just vacated chair in front of the television set, balanced his dinner on his lap and became absorbed in the series of reports of matches that had been played that day.

He finished his food and put the plate at his feet for his mother to pick up and take away. 'Anything else? If not, I'll nip down to our dad,' she said.

Ben shook his dandelion-puff of a head. 'No. Might even see you down there. Some of the lads have got a meet there. There's a special being run up on Saturday for the cup game. We'll probably go mob-handed.'

His mother was now ready to go down and meet Henry. 'Ben, don't think I'm nagging, but I do wish you wouldn't keep pinching the lavatory rolls. It's not nice to keep having someone yelling through the keyhole. If you're not careful, I'll start getting those packs, then you can't take them to your matches.' Although no football fan, she had seen enough on television to know that the rolls were hurled like giant streamers over the tops of the goals.

Ben lied indignantly, 'Look, I don't need to nick them. I can get as many as I like from the public bog.'

She pecked him on his stubbly head. 'I'm not getting on at you. I just don't know what big boys like you see in

11

chucking all those rolls about.'

'You just don't understand. It's all part of the scene.'

Once the door had shut he went into the bathroom and ran a wet flannel over his head, sluiced his face and went into his room to empty his pockets. On the three-ply white-painted chest of drawers he laid out his personal armoury. A chain wrenched from the cistern of a public convenience, some washers with filed edges, a steel comb that served as a face slashing weapon; and almost reverently, a programme from his back pocket which he carefully added to the bedside pile.

It had been a disappointing game in many respects, thought Ben. True his team had won, but there had been no 'aggro', inside or outside the ground. The visiting supporters had arrived and left peaceably, giving no excuse for violence, which was disappointing as there was nothing quite so satisfying as going to bed on a good punch-up. Anyway, home games were always duller. For one thing, you had to watch your step more because there was a real danger of being banned from the ground. If your face was well known as his was, you couldn't get away with much.

Away games were different. First you had the train trips, and they were always good for trouble. Then you had the window smashing rampage through the streets of a town where you were a stranger and in no danger of being identified.

Saturday's away game was a third round cup draw and promised to be a good day out, for tempers became raw-edged at cup time and punch-ups were easy to come by.

Ben and his mates were meeting in the pub to make arrangements for the outing, and already he was tingling with excitement at the prospect of the trouble they planned to cause.

Ben could not rationalise or explain this nihilistic attitude

12

to life, and if questioned about it just shrugged and said, 'It's life,' in just the same way as he passed off his cropped head with, 'The fuzz can't grab hold of it.'

Chapter II

Ben unpadlocked his motor scooter which was secured by a thick chain to some railings at the rear of the flats, and drove three streets away to pick up Jeannie – his 'sort' or 'gimpy'. For that was how he described his girl friend. She was already waiting on the corner; a pale-faced wisp of a girl with dangling earrings and hair cropped short on top, with little kiss-curl bangs on the side, giving her an almost boyish appearance which was enhanced by the faded buttock-hugging blue jeans she was wearing.

Ben revved his 'peanut in a tin' as he stopped beside her.

'Stride,' he shouted above the engine's rattle, and she obediently straddled the pillion seat.

'Hi,' was her sole greeting. As the scooter roared off, Ben made a U-turn without paying any attention to oncoming traffic, then took a corner too wide and so fast that he had to jam his boot on the ground to keep the machine upright. The slipstream set the fox's brush and imitation tiger's tail fluttering boldly behind them, the battery of headlights blinding any approaching driver. Neither wore a protective helmet, for 'skid-lids' were strictly for the chicken hearted, and in any case the exhilaration of scooter riding was lost once the personal risk element was gone. It had to be fast, furious and wind-blown.

The relationship between Ben and Jeannie was a strange one, as neither ever professed affection for the other or gave any physical demonstration of it. It had begun as unromantically as it had remained. It was calculatingly cold, with no concession to soppiness, or 'two penn'orth of hot hand' as they derisively called it. Ben had seen her standing waif-like in a basement disco, gyrating to a blues-beat record, her tiny hips simulating the sex act, her arms jerking backwards and forwards. He had walked with an arrogant cowboy gait across the floor, grabbed her, kissed her roughly, and simply muttered, 'You're mine.' And she was from then on. Jeannie went everywhere with him like a shadow, but not without influence, for she egged him on with a strident voice, and cheered and chanted with him.

She was an accepted member of the gang which followed Ben like sheep, although he had never been appointed leader. It had just emerged that he was their silent spokesman and decision maker. Silent, that is, because Ben could never bother to explain, or attempt to justify, their conduct, although he knew they were constantly under the microscope. Everybody wanted to know what made them tick. Ben knew that they did what they did because they liked it.

'The Penalty Spot' public house they rode to was so close to the Rovers' ground that it actually looked a part of it. Its proximity to the ground had made it a gold mine, and the brewers had cashed in by giving it a distinctly football atmosphere. The saloon bar was called The Free Kick, and the public bar The Throw In.

The interior of the pub – which was run by a former player with ruddy cheeks and a beer pot – was plastered with posters, pennants, rosettes and colour photographs depicting past games and players.

Ben and Jeannie went straight into the public bar and were able to see through to the saloon bar where the older men who supported the team were earnestly replaying the

14

day's game kick by kick. They had been supporters for so long that their knowledge was encyclopaedic. The post mortem was a regular Saturday evening occurrence.

Ben made a grimace of distaste as he heard his father's voice saying sourly, 'I'll give it to you that they won today, but it was more luck than skill, and if you were honest you'd admit it. They need another good striker up front before there's any real hope for them. That's my honest view.'

Henry's contributions were never taken seriously because he was a known knocker who could do nothing but denounce the players and perpetually hark back to the great days of the past.

Ben waited for his father to be ticked off. It came when a grey-faced man banged down his pint of bitter and protested, 'Henry, I don't know how you can sit there and have the nerve to comment. You weren't even at the game.'

Henry, unruffled, said, 'That's why I don't go no longer. The game's finished. I saw it when it was at its best. That's all I'm saying.'

Another voice interrupted. 'But how do you know it's had it when you don't go? Answer me that.'

Henry said, 'I got telly, that's why.' Another voice bellowed, 'Put another record on.'

Ben craned over the bar and shouted, 'Oih, Dad. Who won the cup in 1947? You should remember. That was the last time you saw a ball kicked.'

He roared with laughter, which was taken up by the other men. 'You might as well wrap up, Henry. Ben's got you taped all right,' said the grey-faced man.

Henry just said, 'What's the point of arguing intelligently with the likes of you? Anyone who listens to Ben ain't worth wasting breath on. What's he know about the finer points? Most of the kicking he sees takes place off the field.'

Satisfied he had squashed his father, Ben ordered the drinks – a snowball for Jeannie and whisky mac for himself. Then they fed a fistful of coins into the juke box and made their selection of pop songs, which came out so deafeningly loud that the glasses shook and an elderly couple in the corner were forced to leave.

Gradually the gang drifted into the bar, each arrival heralded by the pop-pop of a scooter. They draped themselves around the room, all individuality erased by the uniformity of their dress, speech and actions.

The only member who stood apart was Wykeham Jefferson Jones. Although he wore the gear, he would always be apart, for he was as brown as coffee. 'Caleb' as the West Indian boy was tagged, was a tearaway with the rest of them, but for a completely different reason. He abhorred violence and the non-stop quest for 'aggro', but he joined in because the gang was the one place where he was unquestioningly accepted. None of them seemed to give a damn about the colour of his skin, and it was worth doing things you disliked just for that. True, Ben could be thoughtless at times, but he never seemed to do it with malice. So Caleb shrugged it off when he was called a Smoked Irishman or Sambo. It was just wonderful to be one of them, and not an outcast like the Paks who nobody seemed to want. He could understand that, because they did make such a point of being different: the women with jewels in their noses and baggy silk pants, and their own cinemas and stinky spice shops. And the men were no different with their continuous bitching about not being allowed to wear turbans on the buses. His own father had had more than his fair share of abuse. It had died down a lot, it was true, but he still remained a partial outcast. Caleb felt he at least had made the break through, and the price was cheap at half the cost.

Some of the boys leaned casually against the wall drinking Coke from punctured tins, while the girls got in the groove by swaying to the music. Others sprawled across the tops of the plain wood tables or stretched full out on the bench seats.

There was no time, however, for them to settle down for Ben suddenly shouted, 'O.K. Let's go,' and headed for the door. There was a deafening roar as the scooters started up, and they drove down the road like riders in a mass start race. Waiting outside were a handful of youngsters not old enough to enter the pub and too young to have scooters, who ran behind shouting and whooping.

The landlord wiped the bar with a wet cloth and said, 'Thank Christ they've gone. One sniff of the barmaid's apron and they're worse than a pack of dervishes.'

Ben led his mob to a basement discotheque that rocked with music, and laid down the plans for the coming match.

'First we want as good a turn-out as possible. This other team have the pottiest load of fans ever. Fanatical sods all of them. Go all over the place. Well, we got to show them we're just as keen and twice as hard.'

There was a chorus of assent, and some of the girls began chanting rhythmically, 'We are the greatest.'

'Put a sock in it,' warned Ben. 'Save it for the game.'

The 'sorts' subsided into giggles.

'One other thing. It's going to cost everyone seventy pence, so those who haven't got it had better do something about it quick. Serious, if you can't raise it, hang around the barrier and we'll try and slip the odd ticket back once we've been through.'

At the end of twenty minutes, Ben had completed his briefing. They would all meet at the station, and once through the barrier pile into the third coach. 'And I don't want no trouble on the way down. Keep it for the return.

Otherwise we might be stopped going into the ground, O.K. If anyone lips you, just swallow it.'

The remainder of the evening passed quickly enough as they danced and went for occasional spins round the houses. The real problem would be filling in time until Rovers met Barnham United on the coming Saturday.

Chapter III

Barry Hudson was looking forward to the game. It could be a classic. Both teams, if they put their minds to it, could play football that was a joy to watch, and by his handling of the game he hoped to promote that. He would be firm but not pernickety. He detested referees who were continually blowing their whistles and whipping out their pencil to book someone for the slightest infringement. A ref could make or mar a game.

The game meant so much to Hudson because it was an important cup match, and one step nearer to his life's ambition – refereeing a Cup Final at Wembley before royalty.

Hudson personified all that was good in football, dedicated but not fanatical, a stickler for the rules and an admirer of the will to win, but not at all costs. Victory should always take second place to sportsmanship. On the other hand, he did not go berserk if he heard a player swear. They were grown men, who shouldn't be ticked off in public like naughty schoolboys. Further, Hudson liked to think the players respected him for it.

Hudson was a little disappointed at the hooligan element that had crept into the game. While he was all for youngsters letting off steam, some of them did tend to overdo it with their disturbing chants when a man was about to take a penalty. And those toilet roll streamers over the goal-post *were* very distracting for the keepers. But, if he was honest with himself, he had seen very little evidence of the violence he was always reading about. Mind you, he was on the field and not the terraces, but he was convinced the papers over-played it. Too many people seemed over-anxious to denigrate the youngsters of today.

It had taken Hudson, who was thirty-six years old, twelve years to reach the position he now held as a referee. It had been a long, hard haul. Promotion had been slow but steady as clubs reported on his handling of games. His record had been good and he had been up-graded through the various amateur leagues to professional soccer, first as a linesman and finally a fully fledged referee.

Although he had a reasonably good job which kept him, his wife and three youngsters (twin sons eight and daughter eleven), quite comfortably, he could easily have bettered himself. He chose, however, to remain in his present job as a factory storekeeper on shift work, because it allowed him the time to referee. And his boss never minded him switching shifts, or his day off, to enable him to pursue his hobby. In fact, it was encouraged because he was such an example to everybody. After having refereed a game he had often gone in and worked the night through.

Barry lived in a three-bedroomed semi-detached house in Swallow Mead, Boxley, the residential area of a new town twenty miles from London. He was buying it on a twenty-five year mortgage. It was ideally situated, for it was far enough away from the centre of London for him to referee games involving London teams. Swallow Mead was typical suburbia, but when he heard it described as such Hudson took neither offence nor exception. It was all he ever wanted. True, most of the residents were a little aloof. Not snobbish or stand-offish; they just liked to keep themselves to themselves. Greetings were exchanged over lawn mowers, or during hedge-clipping or bedding-out sessions, but prolonged discussions were not encouraged. At the moment, life was certainly good for Hudson.

Now he was sitting in his slippers by the open fire which was throwing out a comforting warm glow. His wife Nan was knitting a roll-neck pullover. For Barry, it was the best part of the day. The twins were fast asleep in their double tier bunks and the little girl was whispering prayers with heavy-lidded eyes. They had had their bedtime story read to them. Now the time had come for him and his wife to relax.

'You will come to the game, Nan, won't you?'

'If you really want me to, although you know it's a lot of double dutch to me.'

'I appreciate that, but it'll be a big day for me, love. They're forecasting a 40,000 gate.'

'All right, I'll make it 40,001, but you'll have to get your Mum over to sit in.'

'You'll be really comfortable, Nan. No standing in the cold. I can get you a seat in the directors' box. How's that for influence?'

The time passed quickly. There wasn't even any need for them to talk they were so happy with each other's company.

The clock in the hall chimed ten and Nan yawned, put her knitting away in a bag, and said, 'I'm going up.'

'I'll join you.'

'Haven't you forgotten something, Barry?'

'No. Leastways, I don't think so.'

'Your run.'

'Oh. I'll skip it tonight. Bit tired. I'll get up early instead.'

A regular run was part of Barry's keep fit ritual for he

firmly believed that a referee should be capable of keeping up with the play for a full ninety minutes. So morning or evening, depending on his shift, he put on a tattered track-suit to jog trot down the road to the common, where he ran five miles – much to the amusement of his neighbours. But Barry was oblivious of their stares. Quite apart from its being necessary, he really enjoyed it. With a bit of luck he could keep on until he was forty-seven. Which was another reason why he didn't smoke and drank very little.

Nan padded up the stairs calling as she went, 'Turn the lights out, and don't forget to lock up.'

As Barry went round the house seeing everything was secured, he reflected how lucky he was to have a girl like Nan. Most women nagged hell out of their husbands for giving up too much time to their hobbies. Nan, on the other hand, encouraged him; although she did not like the game she tolerantly complied with his wishes.

When he entered the bedroom he was warm with desire for her. Nan knew this and was waiting. She could read him like a book. A bit tired! What a silly excuse. He only had to ask, she thought, as they embraced.

As he turned over to sleep Barry suddenly shivered.

'What's the matter?' asked Nan.

'Nothing. Someone just walked over my grave,' he said.

Chapter IV

As the hands on the face of the clocking-off machine jerked upright to the vertical position denoting it was exactly noon, Ben was waiting with his time card as if there wasn't a second to waste. Jeannie was already on the corner, a huge rosette fluttering on her breast, and a long scarf wound round her neck like a sleeping python. The names of all the players in the team had been sewn on to the scarf in inch long white stitches.

'What kept you?' she asked.

'Couldn't nip out quicker, the bloody foreman's got eyes in the arse of his trousers.'

He looked over his shoulder, grabbed her arm and started yanking her along the pavement. 'Come on, we'll hop on this one.' Behind them loomed the bulky red shape of a bus. They sprinted a hundred yards to a request stop, and panting heavily just managed to flag it down. Ben handed over his money and let Jeannie pay her own fare to the Underground station four hundred yards along the road. There they caught a tube train to the railway terminal from where the soccer special was leaving.

It was a sharp morning, but dry and bright, which was disappointing to them.

'If it stays like this they won't need the bloody floods till the last fifteen minutes,' said Ben rattily.

There was no need for further explanation. Jeannie knew exactly why his voice expressed dismay. When the stadium darkened and the floodlights were switched on, it was like sitting in a cinema: no one could see the audience, which meant they could set about their mischief without being too closely observed.

As they clumped heavy-booted into the main hall of the station, distorted brass band music was being blared out over the loudspeaker. Pigeons were hopping around between the hard-backed benches, and beside the food vending machines, pecking at the discarded bits of sandwich and food scraps that had been dropped by passengers.

From time to time a voice bellowed train information over an amplifier, but the music coupled with the poor

22

enunciation of the woman announcer, made the words inaudible. But Ben was unworried, he knew exactly which platform to head for. Slotted in the Destination Board was a sign: Football Special.

From the corner of his eye he saw several members of the mob loitering about the station, conspicuous in their desire to be unnoticed. But he studiously ignored them. They would all go through the barrier separately, for a whole crowd might arouse the suspicions of the guards and ticket collectors, who, anticipating trouble, might try and stop them boarding.

The gang held back, waiting for Ben and Jeannie to go through first. The collector punched the tickets and said, 'Enjoy the game, son, but don't smash the train up, eh? We're running short.' The feeble joke failed to hide his anxiety.

'Us? We ain't looking for any aggro. Just going along to cheer, mate.'

'Wish I could join you. Should be a great game.'

They clambered into the third coach, lit cigarettes and waited for the others to join them. The far end of the coach was already packed with a group of middle-aged men who were obviously travelling as a party. They were deep in loud conversation about the game, explaining the tactics the Rovers should adopt if they were to win, the excitement already apparent in their voices. It was informative talk, but the tobacco haze and the stub-littered floor were give-away indications that they were lacking any real confidence. There was a tangible air of wishful thinking.

'Hi, Ben. Hi, Jeannie.'

Ben glanced at the seat opposite and saw Caleb had seated himself there. The coloured boy offered a packet of cigarettes and Ben held up the one between his two fingers to indicate he already had a weed on. It irritated him how

23

Caleb always made a bee-line for the nearest seat to him, or always contrived to be standing alongside on the terrace. Ben wondered if the nig-nog was bent. He certainly went out of his way to get close. Be following me into the bog next, he thought. It did not occur to him that it was a simple case of hero worship or that Caleb knew he would always be accepted if he was at Ben's right elbow.

'I reckon we'll give them a good run for their money, Ben.'

'We will if the dozy sods pull their fingers out. They've been playing like a load of berks lately. Still, if they get stuck in they might throw the others. They don't like hard tackling. A few real crunchy ones could do it and throw them right off their stride. They can't play their arty-farty stuff if they think their shins are going to be caved in every time they get possession.'

A guard with a whistle in his mouth and a green flag at the ready was striding up and down the platform testing door-handles and looking at the big station clock. Ben looked quickly round the carriage, did some head counting and saw that the mob had turned up in full strength. The whistle blew, a brake hissed steam and the train juddered back a foot before it began to move up the platform. The Special was on its way and the relief could almost be touched. The whole train had been apprehensive that some last-minute hitch would cause it to be cancelled. As it gathered momentum, the boys began to sing 'You'll never walk alone' at the tops of their voices. Ben let them carry on. You didn't get chucked off a train for singing, he reckoned. Not even by British Rail.

As the Special rattled on, they sang through their repertoire of songs, some bawdy, some gushingly sentimental. The songs had no local significance and were sung on terraces from Dorset to Doncaster.

24

The town they were travelling to was only thirty miles from London, and less than three quarters of an hour later they were juddering into the glass-domed, soot-grimed station. The platform walls were covered with slogans from aerosol paint-sprays, forecasting inevitable victory for United. Ben waited on the platform until the gang were all together, then marched them solidly towards the barrier. There was no point now in pretending they weren't together as they could not possibly be sent back.

Ben's force totalled thirty strong and formed a solid phalanx as they marched through the streets to the ground. Pedestrians approaching took one look at them, saw their forbidding boots, and promptly crossed to the other side of the road.

With Ben as leader, they kept up a non-stop chorus of singing and chanting: 'We are the greatest' – 'We shall, we shall, we shall not be moved' – 'When the saints go marching in'.

Everything they sang or chanted had a note of menacing defiance about it, and many local inhabitants shook their heads knowingly and forecast trouble before the night was out.

As the thousands of fans approached the stadium, it seemed as if the whole world was converging on it. What had been a fast walk was reduced to a shuffling, pushing crawl. There was no question of going against the tide of people that swept everything with it. Feet were crushed and the task of remaining upright became the major consideration.

The pavement and kerbs were jammed with men behind steaming trolleys shouting 'Hotdogenunions', 'Get your Coke here', 'Hot pie and eels', while men with huge sandwich-boards covered with striped favours competed with vendors who were selling car-key rings with miniature foot-

25

ballers attached. Ticket touts were popping up everywhere with fistfuls of tickets obtained from some never-to-be-revealed source, while newspaper sellers rushed to and fro with bundles of special colour-supplements under their arms trying to out-shout their competitors.

Ben paused long enough to buy four tins of Coke.

Mounted police on big horses that snorted and frothed at the mouth as they tossed their heads, were edged sideways through the crowd in an attempt to keep it mobile. Some people living in the road leading to the stadium had fool-ishly left their cars parked outside, so that fans finding their paths blocked clambered thoughtlessly over the roofs, which clanged alarmingly as they were dented. A police loudspeaker van in a side street was appealing to deaf ears: 'Don't push. There's plenty of time and plenty of room inside.'

Incredibly, some fathers had children straddled 'flying angel' style around their necks and shoulders. They kept bellowing angrily, 'Go easy for Christ's sake, I've got a kid here.'

Ben led his mob in a concerted surge towards the turn-stile that led to the terrace behind one of the goals. It was at the opposite end to the one local fans had firmly established as their own inviolate territory.

The ends were the most jam-packed parts of the ground, but the people who elbowed for places on them would never dream of going anywhere else. If they had been handed seats in the grandstand they would have scornfully refused them. They would have felt like battle-hungry soldiers being offered a soft number behind the lines.

Once inside, Ben waited for the others to gather around. A hasty muster assured him they were all present. A blue haze was already curling skywards from the thousands of cigarettes being smoked, while in the centre circle of the

26

pitch the town's brass band was playing selections from well-known musical shows; but none of the crowd was paying the slightest heed to their efforts.

When Ben ran up the concrete steps to the terrace behind the goal, he saw that it was already full. It did not seem possible to fit another body in. Drastic action was called for.

A narrow asphalt path separated the terrace from the seats in the goal-mouth stand, while a seven-foot-high plasterboard wall acted as a barrier to stop anyone clambering up into the seats. Ben stood with his back to the wall and shouted. 'Come on. Come on. Drum. Drum.'

As the gang, their faces split with malicious grins, lined up on either side of him, he began a frenzied drumming on the wall with the heels of his boots and the palms of his hands. The others took it up until it sounded as if the stand would crash down from the vibration. Then as suddenly as it had started, it ceased. Ben roared, 'Charge the bastards. Charge.' Jeannie's high-pitched voice repeated the command.

At the signal they hurled themselves with a juddering impact into the backs of the people on the terrace. The momentum forced the crowd to give and stumble down the slope. Scores of people were winded and bruised as they were pinned against the crash barriers. Women screamed hysterically, several people went down on their knees, to be yanked upright by helping hands and just saved from being trampled to death. Those in the front row took the full brunt of the onslaught as their chests crunched against the safety rail fringing the field. A number fainted and were hoisted unceremoniously over the tops of heads, to be laid out on stretchers and revived by the volunteer first-aid men. But the move left a large gap which Ben and the others gleefully took over. There were a few angry exchanges, but they soon dissipated into sullen acceptance that the gang of youths would not give ground. They were there to stay, and nothing short of a pitched battle would dislodge them.

Ben put his four Coke tins on the ground and used them as a stand to give him a vantage view. The band marched off unappreciated and unapplauded.

Suddenly, the vast crowd became mute, then erupted into a lung-straining roar. Thousands of scarves seemed to have been strung together in a continuous line as the fans held them above their heads and swayed sideways in a rhythmical tempo. Seconds later the two teams trotted out from a tunnel below the directors' box.

The stadium was filled with a cacophony of whistles, rubber-bulbed car horns, bugles and wooden rattles. Striped bobble hats were waved as the numbered players did knees-bend exercises, jack-knifed in the air trying to make their knees touch their chests, or simply sprinted on the spot. The two goal-keepers tossed their gloves and caps into a corner of the net and prepared to face a bombardment of limbering-up shots from their own team-mates.

Ben hoisted his right first above his head, looked around and screamed, 'If you hate United – clap,' almost toppling off his tins with the effort. The terrace echoed with the staccato tattoo of clapping as if countless flamenco dancers had suddenly gone berserk.

Barry Hudson, in neatly pressed black jerkin and shorts, trotted to the centre spot and summoned the two captains. One solemnly tossed a penny, and when it hit the ground both bent over to see whether they had been lucky in the call. From his gesture it was apparent that the Rovers' skipper had called correctly and decided to defend the goal which lay below Ben. The practice balls were booted off the pitch and pounced upon by two of the green-bereted boy scouts acting as ball retrievers.

The players changed ends and took up their positions, prancing nervously like horses. A new white ball was placed on the centre spot. Hudson solemnly consulted his pocket-watch, then his wrist-watch, put his whistle in his mouth and blew a long blast. The din that followed could be heard two miles away.

The first few minutes of play were scrappy and untidy, with the tense, nerved-up players being too anxious and impetuous. Both defences started apprehensively so that when their goals were menaced they deliberately kicked the ball out of play, which led to derisive taunts of, 'Keep it on the island'.

Gradually both teams settled down and began to play exciting, attractive football. There were loud 'Oohs', mingling with groans of dismay, at missed opportunities. After twenty minutes the United centre-forward took a long shot at goal which hit the crossbar and bounced out of play. United fans roared, 'Hard luck', while Rovers supporters shouted, 'Jammy sod'. One wag yelled, 'Raise it a foot'.

The first half ended with neither side having scored, and the players traipsed off for a dressing-room pep talk from their respective managers. Hudson went into his dressing-room with the two linesmen. The game was not discussed, but Hudson was more than happy at the way he was handling things. Once when an injured player was receiving treatment from the trainer, he had glanced up into the stand hoping to catch a glimpse of Nan, but all he had seen was a blur of pink faces, banners made from bed sheets bearing black slogans, and a multi-coloured rash of hats, coats and scarves. He knew, however, that Nan could be proud of him, and when the after-match reports were sent in he felt confident they would be flattering.

It was in the twelfth minute of the second half that the first signs of ugliness emerged. The Rovers were sieging

United's goal; repeatedly a goal seemed inevitable, but each time the ball was booted clear by a desperate defender, only to be lobbed back, with heads rising to meet it in a goal-mouth scramble. Then when it looked as if Rovers must score, Hudson blew his whistle and indicated a free kick to the defenders. His sharp eye had spotted one of the Rovers' forwards grabbing an opponent by the back of his jersey. He was thronged by a group of furious remonstrating players, but he was adamant and waved them back with a forceful, sweeping movement of his hand. Then he stood, hands on hips, until the players realised he would not be intimidated into changing his mind.

Livid with anger, Ben chanted, 'Who called the ref a prick?', and immediately the response was shouted, 'Who called the prick a ref?'

A man below Ben turned round and said over his shoulder, 'You blind, son? He almost pulled the shirt off his back.'

'Balls. What does a blind old sod like you know?' And although it reduced his field of visibility, Ben hurled two of the tins of Coke over the heads of the people below, one striking a St John's Ambulance Brigade man on the back with a loud thump, the other landing harmlessly in front of the goal-keeper who kicked it contemptuously over the line and on to the cinder track.

The man below said, 'Knock it off. There's no need for that kind of behaviour.'

Ben said, 'You want duffing up?'

Fear registered on the man's face as he turned and saw the fearsome looks on the faces of the youths behind. One spat in his face and warned, 'We'll see you outside'. A wisp of a girl screamed, 'Nu' him, Ben.'

The man knew enough of the aggro boys' language to know the girl was urging her boy friend to butt him in the face. He decided that he was capable of doing it too, so turned and faced the pitch again; but the rest of the match was spoilt for him. He could not concentrate on what was going on below. All his attention was diverted to what might happen behind him.

The floodlights came on, and from that moment Ben and his friends led a constant barrage of abuse. Whenever an opposition player committed a foul they stamped, and demanded, 'Off. Off. Off.' They did it even when the tackle was quite fair.

To the tune of 'Clementine' they sang:

> *Who's your father?*
> *Who's your father?*
> *Who's your father, referee?*
> *You ain't got one*
> *You're a bastard,*
> *You're a bastard, referee.*

People around them began to try and edge away, sensing the mood of violence that was deliberately fomented. The singing gave way to a monotonous, incessant baying of, 'Hooli – Hooli – Hooli-gans'. A handful of the youths had left the terrace and clambered through the barbed wire encircling the base of the floodlight pylons and were clinging precariously to the angle iron as they skimmed sharp-edged washers into the crowd. Heads bobbed up and down to screams of 'Duck'.

An enormous roar that was so loud it even deafened the chanting of the youths, enveloped the ground. Rovers' goal was once again under assault. Suddenly the referee's whistle trilled above the noise.

United's centre-forward lay prostrate on the ground, writhing and groaning, and frantically tearing down his right stocking. A trainer with a sponge was already sprinting across the pitch. Hudson, ringed by a circle of gesticulating players, was pointing to the penalty spot. His forefinger stabbed again and again at the whitewash blob as he ordered the players back with his other hand. It looked for one moment as if blows would be struck as United players joined the melee, and tried to impress on the Rovers' players that they were being ridiculous in objecting to the referee's decision.

Hudson, ball under his arm, made it clear that he would not alter his decision, and the players reluctantly moved away, leaving the solitary figure of the goal-keeper poised cat-like to leap as the kick was taken. But the ball was in the back of the net before he had even moved. The stadium erupted.

Ben and his followers hurled streams of obscene abuse at the referee and tried to force a path through the crowd and invade the pitch, but the crowd in front was so dense that even their concerted shoving had no effect.

Suddenly Hudson was checking on his two watches. His whistle went to his mouth and a long piercing blast indicated that it was all over. The players moved about shaking each other's hands before racing off the field. A cordon of police formed around the perimeter, and by the time anyone had forced their way on to the pitch the players, referee and linesmen were all safely down the tunnel.

Ben and his gang found themselves being propelled backwards as the people in front of them turned and began to force their way towards the exits. Ben became isolated from his friends and jumped up and down yelling, 'Everyone to the players' entrance.' Powerless against the crowd, he allowed himself to be propelled towards the exit, determined to wreak vengeance on somebody once he was outside.

32

Chapter V

Barry Hudson was towelling himself after a hot bath when a uniformed police inspector, peaked cap under his left arm and brown gloves in his right hand, walked into the steam-filled room.

'How are you proposing to get home, sir?' he enquired.

'By car of course. I drove over.'

'I think it might be wiser and better for all concerned if you let us run you home,' he said.

'But my wife is with me,' said Hudson, who automatically wondered what he had done wrong, for he was one of those people whose pulse-rate went up and a feeling of guilt invaded him even when he saw a police car in his driving mirror.

'That's all right. We'll find room for her, and naturally see your car is delivered safely,' said the inspector. Then sensing the unease his appearance had caused, added, 'There's no cause for alarm, sir.' But his tone lacked conviction and did nothing to dispel Hudson's unease. He wondered why policemen always sounded so menacingly aggressive even when they were trying to help.

Hudson made a feeble gesture of protest. 'I fail to see the need for this ...' he began, but the words petered out when he was interrupted.

'There's a crowd of yobos outside the players' entrance. We keep dispersing them but they drift back.' The inspector smacked his gloves against the palm of his left hand. 'Could do them for obstruction, but we'd look a bit silly if it turned out they only wanted to see the teams leave. My

33

own view though is they'll be violent. That's why I'm taking these precautions.'

Hudson, irritable with himself for suddenly being dry-mouthed and anxious, said, 'But why on earth should they want to get at me? Thank you for your offer, Inspector, but I'll drive home. I've had no trouble with youngsters in the past.' Then seeing the expression of annoyance on the officer's face, added hastily, 'I think it would distress my wife unduly. So if you don't mind.'

'It's not a question of my minding or not minding. I can't force you into doing anything against your will. Sorry I've troubled you.' Whereupon he about-turned smartly, rammed on his cap and strode out.

It took Hudson twenty minutes to dress and fold his kit into the zip-topped holdall, by which time he was fully composed and relaxed. When he met his wife, she kissed him with a stamp of approval and said, 'You were wonderful, darling. I'm so proud. You clever boy.'

Barry tried to disguise his pleasure. 'Don't go potty, love. It's just another game, let's face it.'

'I don't care. I don't think anyone could have done it better.'

'Knock it off, love. You'll be giving me a big head.'

'And you deserve it. Let's find the car and go home. Mum's put a casserole on and I'm starving. I phoned in the intermission and the kids have been as good as gold.'

He did not have the heart to correct her by saying half-time. She gave him such a glow he even forgot to mention the inspector's call.

A straight-backed veteran in the dark blue uniform of the Royal Corps of Commissionaires opened the gates to let them out. 'Watch your step, sir. One or two ugly little buggers around tonight. Begging your pardon, madam,' he said as he noticed the woman passenger.

34

'I don't think they've got a bone to pick with me,' said Barry as he passed a silver ten penny piece through the window. He eased into first gear and peered anxiously through the windscreen. But he could see nothing ominous.

Although an economy-minded engineer had doused the floodlights and the street ahead was sparsely lit by lamp standards, visibility was not all that poor, and he could see nothing ahead to alarm him.

'The old, old story. Seeing rocks ahead when there aren't any.'

'And just what was that in aid of?' asked Nan.

'Nothing, darling. Merely thinking aloud.'

Then as he flicked the dash-board switch to put his head-lamps at the dipped position, he picked out some blurred shapes on the pavement. As he got closer he saw groups of youngsters, but they didn't look as if they were mobilised for trouble. Probably autograph hunters or soccer-crazy kids who would wait hours just to slap a player on the shoulder and have the impertinence to mention his christian name with the familiarity of a long established friend.

'Darling, do let's get a move on. We haven't got all night,' rebuked Nan. He accelerated, but something seemed to have suddenly gone wrong. The indistinct shapes appeared to be assembling as a solid unit across the road directly in his path. The tiny blue beam-light on the dash-board lit up as he put the headlamps full on, and he re-coiled with a jolt as he saw a row of crop-haired youths and girls stretched like a barrier ahead. As he sounded his horn in a long blast, he felt Nan's hand tighten on his bicep.

'What do they want?'

'Nothing. Just slip down on to the floor. It's nothing to worry about,' he said. He lowered his window and shouted, 'Come on now, make way.' His voice was as firm as the one adopted to order demonstrating players back to their positions, but it immediately became obvious that in this situation his word was not final.

A girl's voice screamed, 'That's him, Ben. That's the bastard.'

Hudson went into second gear and accelerated sharply, but the car was suddenly encircled by a horde of screaming hooligans, their faces contorted with fury.

'Get out, you fucker,' screamed a youth who seemed to be the leader. Another said, 'You wanker,' and indulged in a masturbatory gesture. Solid boots thudded against the bodywork, and a crescendo of blows rained down on the roof and bonnet, various objects began to thump against the windows, and the car began to rock on its springs as the youths tried to turn it over.

'Drive through them,' screamed Nan.

'I daren't. One of them might go under the wheels.'

'That's just too bloody bad.' Even in that moment of peril he felt annoyance and surprise at Nan using such unaccustomed language. But it was a momentary diversion, for too late he realised that his window was open and one boy was leaning through trying to snatch the ignition keys. Hudson pummelled at the grasping hand with a clenched fist and shouted, 'For God's sake be sensible before somebody gets hurt.' A washer struck him above the eye making a deep-lipped cut, drawing a thin trickle of blood. The nearside headlamp splintered. Someone shouted, 'Let his soddin' tyres down.'

'Don't you dare,' he roared, realising that only mobility stood between them and serious injury. Then dark shapes, taller and bulkier, shouldered into the crowd; youths and girls were yanked away from the car, and Hudson could see them being tossed unceremoniously into a blue windowless van which seemed to have appeared from nowhere. The rocking ceased. A familiar face in a peaked cap peered

36

through the window.

'Put your foot down and leave the rest to us. It's a pity, sir, that you didn't take more kindly to well-intentioned advice. We could have avoided all this.' There was a sharp thump on the roof. On your way, and you'd better get that eye seen to. And an anti-tetanus jab.'

Hudson drove the car at full speed, not even bothering to halt at the major road ahead; the tyres screeched as he made a sharp left hand turn, filling the interior with the smell of burning rubber. His own hands were shaking violently, and Nan was cowering on the floor sobbing. He meant to pat her back in a solacing gesture, but he struck her on the head. 'Not to worry, love. We're well clear now. Let's stop for a coffee down the road.'

'No. If you're all right I'd prefer to go straight home. I feel rather sick. I'll tell you one thing though: I'll recognise one of them anywhere. The coloured one. He was screaming louder than the rest put together. Not that I heard what he yelled, but he was obviously egging them on.'

Ben realised the police had taken control of the situation, and as he watched the rear lights of the intended victim's car disappear he shouted, 'Scapa. Everyone scapa.'

The police were still bundling people into the van. Those who struggled were hoisted in by the seat of the pants and scruff of the collars, and any who tried to kick their way free were deprived of their status symbol boots. Ben's anger mounted at what he considered was lousy deceit on the part of the fuzz, who had given the impression of dispersing, but had obviously re-formed in a side street ready to pounce. It was a typically bastard copper trick. Anyway, the lousy ref had got away, so there was no point in loafing around and getting knocked off. He looked anxiously around for Jeannie, but she was not to be seen; only Caleb was near at hand.

'You're a right shit,' he told the coloured boy. 'Whose bloody side you on, anyway? Just when it looks like we've got that robbing bastard ref, you start yelling your bonce off for everyone to go easy.'

'Ben, I was in there with you and the lads, it's just that I thought it was getting out of hand. We didn't want anyone to get real hurt, surely?'

'Since when you been running things, Caleb? You know you ain't black, you're yellow.' And he spat contemptuously on the pavement. He didn't see the hurt in the coloured youth's eyes.

By now the police had formed an arm-linked cordon across the road, and were advancing steadily towards the locked stadium gates, so that anyone who did not escape would be caught like sardines in a net.

Chapter VI

The only avenues of escape remaining were down the narrow side streets, and it was along these that the youths began to flee. Over his shoulder Ben caught a glimpse of Jeannie still defying the police and shouting abuse. Doubling back, he grabbed her arm and tugged her protesting towards one of the intersecting roads. 'Don't be a daft bitch, or do you want your hair parted by a bloody truncheon? They can be violent sods when they get going.'

The street echoed with the thud-thud-thud of the heavy boots of the escaping rowdies; but there was no panic in their running. They were still laughing and enjoying the escapade. All, that is, except Caleb who, pounding beside

Ben, was trying desperately to explain his position. 'You've got it all wrong about me, Ben,' he panted. 'I was right in there with you.'

'You're chicken shit,' sneered Ben. While Jeannie scornfully told him, 'Don't know why you bother to come if you don't enjoy it.'

As they fled the air was filled with the shatter of broken milk bottles which they kicked whenever they found them lined up outside front doors. They passed warehouses as gaunt as prisons, and skirted a brewery that gave off the sweet cloying smell of yeast; then over a wooden footbridge that spanned a canal.

By repeatedly backdoubling and avoiding the main streets, they managed to reach the station without being halted and questioned by the police. When they entered the station and saw squads of officers standing in groups around the platforms they became transformed and walked to their train in an orderly, well-behaved manner that aroused no suspicions at all. They were still game for a bit more fun, but there was no point in taking chances with the consequent risk of a stiff fine at the magistrates court.

They headed leisurely and meekly for the coach they had agreed upon before leaving London, and as they slumped into the seats sending up puffs of dust, Ben thumped his knees and shouted, 'What a giggle! Did you see the look on the face of that poor old bloody ref? It was worth it just for that.'

Caleb said rather solemnly, 'I only hope he didn't see our faces, Ben.'

'Blimey, there you go again. You're a real dampener and no mistake. What difference does it make, for Christ's sake. In that light all faces look the same. He'd never get away with a firm. ident. Not in a million years.'

Caleb did not voice his own fear that *his* face did not

look just like the rest. It was agonisingly outstanding. Still, he had been trying to stop them, and surely that would stand in his favour if anything went wrong.

In dribs and drabs they piled slowly into the coach, quickly resuming their pummeling and jostling, but it was apparent that their numbers were greatly reduced.

'Where's everybody?' enquired Ben. 'We came here mob-handed, now look at us.'

'Dunno,' said one youth. 'Some got nicked 'cos I saw them hoiked into the meat barrow by the ground.'

A girl in bell-bottom slacks said indifferently, 'Some got knocked off in the High Street for smashing a shop window and chucking some dustbins in the road.'

'Serves the daft buggers right,' said Ben. 'Some of them don't know when they've had enough. Not like Caleb here. He's had enough before he's even started.'

Caleb flushed unnoticeably, produced his cigarettes and handed them around saying, 'Ben, I wish you would listen. I'd like to explain. Put the record straight kind of.' But a whistle sounded, and Jeannie said, 'We're off. The fuzz can't touch us now.'

They leant back and relaxed, then sat bolt upright as the carriage door thumped open and two young men in their early twenties flopped breathlessly on to a three-space seat. They were dressed in the height of current fashion, neat reefer-style jackets, sharply creased trousers with flared bottoms and multi-coloured ties. Their hair was long but tidy, and brushed to a gloss.

'Phew, just made it, John.'

John loosened his tie. 'Bit of a mad rush, Michael, We shouldn't have stopped for a drink. Cutting it too fine.'

Ben, who was looking at them along the passageway between the seats, mimicked in a mincing voice, 'We shouldn't have stopped for a drink, Michael.'

But the two young men studiously ignored him and began to engage in earnest conversation about the match. 'Pity we lost, but there it is. Someone has to,' said John. 'Our turn will come, don't worry.'

'We didn't disgrace ourselves, that's the main thing,' said his friend.

Ben rose from his seat and confronted them. 'You can hop it to another coach. We don't want any long-haired artie-farties in with us.'

John looked astonished. 'I beg your pardon?'

'I beg your pardon,' mocked Ben. 'You deaf or something? We don't want long-haired layabouts in our coach,' he said with menacing provocation.

Michael said, 'And we don't want any trouble. We've just had an enjoyable afternoon watching football. If you want us to move that's all right by us. Come on, John.'

The two men rose to go, but Ben pushed John back in his seat. Michael obediently resumed his.

'What's wrong with us? Don't you like our company? Ain't we good enough?' said Ben. 'I'd have thought you would have loved getting stuck in a carriage full of blokes.'

'Look,' said John, 'We are more than happy to go or stay. It's immaterial to us.'

'I don't like the way you say that. You are talking as if I need to be humoured. It's not like that at all. It's up to me what you do.'

'This is ridiculous,' snorted Michael, and in an attempt to dismiss Ben's presence, he said to John, 'I honestly think we could have pulled it off if our forwards had been a little more aggressive.'

'Don't try and pretend we're not here,' said Ben. 'Anyway, what do you know about football?'

'Nothing, if you say so,' said Michael in a patient voice.

'Don't you try and lip me,' shouted Ben. 'That's a dead

cert way of starting the aggro.'

'Leave it to me, Mike,' said John. 'Look, we aren't looking for trouble. That's the last thing we want. Just let us both go next door.'

'No, we like needling you. It's a giggle.'

'I'm afraid in that case you're wasting your time. We won't be provoked.'

'Oh, we are getting posh with our words, aren't we?'

John stood up. 'We've had enough of this,' he said. 'Whether you like it or not, we're going.'

'But we want you to stay,' said Ben. 'Don't we?' His followers bellowed a lusty, 'Yes,' and began encircling the two men whose faces were beginning to register acute fear.

'We don't like the way you think our team was fairly beaten. We don't think they were. Do we lads?'

The roar, 'No,' drowned the noise of the train.

'It's only a game, after all,' said John feebly.

'Oh, no, that's where you're wrong. So very wrong.' Ben shook his head in an admonishing gesture. 'You play to win.'

Michael said, 'Of course you do, but if you are fairly and squarely beaten that's an end to it.'

'But we wasn't. We had a bent ref against us. Anyway, what kind of fans are you that won't stick up for your own team? That's being a traitor.'

'We're as loyal as the next person,' said Michael.

'Now, that we just can't have,' said Ben. 'We don't like our loyalty questioned by strangers.'

'This is quite ridiculous,' pleaded a completely perplexed John. 'Everything we say is wrong.'

'That is what he's been trying to tell you,' said Jeannie, bursting into excited little giggles.

The two men looked at each other, anxiously seeking guidance, but they could see no way out of their predicament, for they were unable to fathom the workings of the minds of these strange youths who seemed intent on contradicting everything they said.

Michael, his irritation eroding his caution, protested angrily, 'We're not cowards, if that's what you think. But we'd be damned stupid to do anything outnumbered six to one.'

'Oh, if that's what's narking you don't worry,' said Ben. 'We can get round that all right. Caleb! Here.'

'Yes, Ben.'

'These two are worried that we'll duff them up mob-handed. We won't do no such thing. You just take that John and sort him out ... good and proper.'

'What do you want me to do, Ben?'

'Please yourself, nut him, boot him, chin him. Anything you like. Just show him we don't need backing up.'

'Ben, he hasn't done anything. What's the point? What's it prove?' pleaded Caleb.

'It's not meant to prove anything. Why should it? Just thump the bastard. He's the one who's spoiling for a punch-up. Man to man he wants it. You heard him. Well, he's got it.'

Michael said in a quavering voice, 'I'm warning you all. If this intimidation goes on I won't hesitate to pull the communication cord. Then you'll all be in real trouble.'

Ben hit him so hard in the mouth that he gashed his knuckles, then he grabbed his lapels, pulled him forward and butted him across the bridge of the nose, sending out a spume of blood. As Michael fell to the floor, Ben kicked him three times in the stomach and groin.

The vicious assault seemed the signal for the others to go wild. Chrome-barred luggage racks were wrenched from the walls, and heaved through the coach windows. Jeannie and three boys burst into the lavatory and forced the

43

pedestal off its anchoring bolts and tossed it out through the lowered window of the door. Seats were ripped open and the stuffing set alight. Passengers shouted, 'For God's sake knock it off. Someone'll get seriously injured.' Some turned their backs on the fracas and fled through the communicating doors into adjoining carriages.

John was kneeling on the floor tending his injured friend. 'Take him, Caleb,' ordered Ben.

'I can't. I just can't. They've had more than enough.'

The threat galvanised the stunned John into action and he yanked desperately at the communication cord. 'I want a doctor,' he screamed.

'You daft bugger, Caleb. Now we're really in trouble,' muttered Ben.

John was whimpering, 'Please don't hit me. Please. Just leave us alone.'

Caleb looked down at the motionless Michael and said in a subdued voice, 'You've done it this time, Ben. He's dead.'

'Balls. He's all right. A kick in the goolies and a nut in the kisser don't kill anyone. Look, you can see him breathing. So stop worrying and don't lose your bottle.'

The train jerked and juddered, throwing them off their feet as the emergency brakes were applied. It stopped in a high-banked cutting, and when Ben pushed his head out of a broken window he could see the guard striding down the rails towards a track-side telephone. The driver was close behind him. Heads were poking out from other windows, and voices were demanding, 'What the hell's going on?'

'I don't know about you lot,' said Ben. 'But this little how's your father is a bit too much. I'm off. Come on, Jeannie.'

Ben opened a door and stood balanced on the balls of his feet; the ground below looked a frighteningly long way away. 'It's a long way to Tipperary,' he bellowed, then

44

jumped. As he hit the ground he rolled over, then stood ready to catch Jeannie as she stood in the open doorway like a parachutist about to jump. The guard was holding the phone in one hand and blowing frantic blasts from a whistle held in the other. The driver had broken into a jog trot.

'Jump, for crissake,' yelled Ben.

Jeannie jumped. Hands high above her head. He cushioned the fall which knocked him over, and they both rose laughing. Then they scrambled hand in hand up the embankment, through a back garden and into a road. Several others had joined them, and in the road Ben paused just long enough to say, 'We'll have to split up and find our own way back. If you're stopped act dumb and give a false name and address.'

Ben and Jeannie ran until they reached a main road. In the distance they could hear the yowl and barking of police dogs.

'Jesus, they rounded the dogs up sharpish.'

Ben waited off the road while Jeannie thumbed for lifts. When a lorry stopped to pick her up, he appeared as if from nowhere to join her.

The disappointment registered on the driver's face. 'I thought you was alone,' he said. 'Anyway, hop in the pair of you. Not that it matters. She looks young enough to be jail bait.'

They explained that they were hard-up students who were making their way home for a short vacation. The look the driver gave them expressed his total disbelief, but he kept chatting, only too pleased to have company on the last leg of a long and tiring journey. He dropped them at a lorry drivers' pull-up cafe conveniently close to an Underground station. 'This is as far as I go, kids. Have fun.'

Ben and Jeannie thanked him, caught a tube and went home.

There was still a fair amount of telly viewing left. With a bit of luck the day's escapade would be mentioned. Both felt it had been far too successful to be ignored.

Chapter VII

As the crippled train drew into the main line station, batches of policemen were waiting to interview the occupants about the vandalism. Despite the on-the-spot search when the train had been halted, nothing of value had been elicited from the passengers who solemnly swore they had not seen a thing; while the damaged carriage when boarded had been deserted except for the injured Michael and his distraught friend. And all he could say was that the man who struck his friend had jumped out. So, too, had a coloured youth he was sure he could identify again. As the train was shunted to the next station where an ambulance was waiting, a police officer took John the whole length of the train, but he was unable to identify anyone. For, as he rather apologetically explained, 'They all look so alike. Except the coloured boy, of course.'

As for the youths questioned, they had all emphatically denied ever having been in the damaged coach, and they brought forward friends to vouch for it.

A search of nearby streets had also proved negative. Some kids, number uncertain, had been seen running away but there was no sign of them now. Reluctantly, the driver had been allowed to complete his journey to London.

On the station platform, large posters had been hastily set up on trestles. They offered a £50 reward to anyone giving information that would lead to the arrest and conviction of the vandals. It was a tempting sum, but people who had witnessed the havoc walked past with unseeing eyes, and at the barrier they remained tight-lipped to questioners. It was a railway matter, or for the police to sort out. Anyway, they pointed out to each other, who ever heard of anyone actually getting a reward. Lawyers drew up the posters with deliberate loopholes so they could dodge forking out any cash.

'That you, Little Ben?' called his mother as she heard the key grate in the lock. 'You're late, love. Anything wrong?' It was a rhetorical question, for long experience had taught her not to expect a reply.

Ben slouched into the sitting room, went straight across to the television set, switched it on, then flopped into a chair.

'Any grub, Mum?'

'Don't tell me you've gone all this time without a bite to eat. You'll ruin your health, boy.'

'Now, what chance did I have? I went straight from work to the match. Didn't I?' he said surlily.

'I'm not getting on at you, son. I just wish you'd take better care. Eggs, chips and beans do you?'

'It'll do. And a tin of beer if the old man's left any.'

'I'll see,' she said, scurrying into the kitchen as if obeying a royal dictate. She called through the door, 'I hope you weren't mixed up in any of that football nonsense they were talking about in the news. You could get hurt with some of those awful people.'

'Don't worry about me, Mum. I can look after myself.'

'You may think you can, but youngsters who can do that kind of thing to a railway carriage can get up to anything. Don't know what makes them do it. It's a problem, I do declare.'

She came in with the food and took the chair opposite. 'Tell me about the game, Ben. Enjoy it?'

'Not much of a game to be frank. We lost, but only because the ref had been got at. Someone backhanded him all right.'

'What a shame. Still, never mind. They'll be playing again next week.'

'Yes, but not in the Cup, Mum.'

'You see any of this trouble on the train?'

'No, we believe in keeping ourselves to ourselves and minding our own business. Where's the old man?'

'He should be in soon. He had the chance of a few hours overtime, and on his money you can imagine how grateful he was for that. Expect he stopped for a pint before coming home. No one can say he don't deserve it.'

Even after such a short time in the house, Ben was feeling restless and bored with his mother's conversation, so he hid his head behind a sporting magazine. But she, who had been alone all day, was anxious for someone to talk to, the subject did not matter. It was just the sheer pleasure of hearing another voice.

'You go with that girl friend of yours?'

'She's not my bird. Just one of the gang.'

'I bet she wouldn't thank you if she heard herself talked about like that. She looks a sweet little thing.'

'She's all right.'

'Why don't you ever ask her round? You're not ashamed of us, are you?'

'Now why should I be ashamed to bring her here? She don't live in no palace herself, Mum. Her dad works like everybody else's.'

'Well, do bring her round. I would like to get to know her. There's nothing nicer I think than a fellow having a pretty girl and going steady. Keeps his feet on the ground.

Go on – for your Mum, Ben.'

'O.K. I'll ask her to come in tomorrow afternoon. We can watch the match on the goggle box. It's being shown then.'

'Lovely. I'll cut some nice sandwiches. Maybe your Dad would like to watch it too.'

'I don't mind, but it'll be wasted on him. He'd be better off with, "Those were the Days".'

Half an hour later, Henry came in whey-faced with fatigue, but cheerful at the extra money he had earned. 'Hullo, May. Ben. Enjoy the game? Bit of trouble on the way back from what I hear. You're in my seat, Ben.'

Ben rose obediently, for even he acknowledged that the armchair was used by no one other than his father when he was at home.

'Ben's bringing his girl friend around tomorrow,' said May, the pleasure evident in her voice. 'It'll be nice to have a young girl to talk to.'

'That the one you usually cart around, Ben? Looks a nice kind of youngster to me. As I earned a few extra bob, I'll get some beer in. It's time you had a steady girl. Keep you out of mischief.'

'I don't need no girl to keep an eye on me, Dad. And if you carry on like that any more, I won't bring her round, so please yourself.'

'Your Dad's only joking, Ben. Don't be so touchy.'

Henry winked across the room at his wife. 'You know something, May, I think he's a bit soft on her. Still, mustn't rib you too much. Hard luck you lost, but to be honest I never thought you were in it with a chance. That's why I didn't bother to go. You see, son, they just don't have the striking power up front, too much defence in depth. I remember the great Ted Drake, brilliant opportunist, netting nine goals against Sunderland. When you've seen that kind of genius, you don't go trotting off to watch third-raters perform.'

'Get your facts right for once. It was *seven* and it was *Aston Villa*, not Sunderland. And if you want to know, it was December 14th 1935 at Birmingham.'

'All right. I made a slight slip, but you don't have to be so bolshie about it. Your hackles go right up at the least little thing.'

'It ain't that, Dad, and you know it. You must make yourself a laughing stock. Keep your mouth shut if you can't take the trouble to get things right.'

'Sorry I spoke, I'm sure,' he said huffily. 'Just because I don't go around bashing people about don't mean I can't talk about football, does it? Or has a new law been passed?'

May interrupted them. 'For heaven's sake pack it up you two. You can't have a pleasant chat without being at each other like cat and dog.'

Ben stood up. 'He started it. He's still living in the Middle Ages.'

'And thank God I am. In those days players didn't run around with hair round their shoulders.'

'What on earth's that got to do with it?'

'Everything,' said his father with a note of finality. 'Just about everything.'

'Oh, wrap up. If you want to see some real football, watch tomorrow afternoon. You can also see how we were diddled. I'm off to bed.'

'You do just that,' snapped his father, as if Ben was running away from the inescapable logic of his argument. 'Go on, put your head in the sand. Be an ostrich.'

May rounded on them both. 'There are times when I wish football had never been invented. It certainly don't do anything for this house.'

When Ben reached his room, he put the match pro-

gramme on top of the bedside pile and neatly tapped the
edges until they were perfectly aligned. Then he clambered
into bed and slept through the night in a deep, untroubled
slumber.

Chapter VIII

Barry Hudson drove up to his house, and Nan could barely
wait for him to apply the handbrake before rushing indoors
and up the stairs to see her soundly sleeping children.

When Barry had finished parking the car, he went in and
greeted his mother and asked, 'Kids been any trouble?'

'No. Good as gold, but then they always are. What on
earth has got into Nan? She went up the stairs like a
scalded cat. The times I've sat in you'd think she would
trust me by now.'

'It's not that. We had a bit of bother on the way home; I
think she's still a bit shaken up.'

Barry crossed over to the sideboard and took out a bottle
of whisky, held it up to the light and said, 'Still a little left
over from Christmas. Fancy a nip, Mum?'

'Don't mind if I do, Barry, but what's the celebration
for? Not at all like you to tipple without good excuse.'

He took out three glasses and tipped a modest amount of
whisky into each. When Nan came in she flounced into a
chair and giggled nervously. 'All right, don't any of you say
it. I'm acting like a ninny.'

Barry handed her a drink. 'Just knock that back, love.
You'll feel better. Great nerve steadier they tell me.'

'I do wish one of you would let me know what's going
on,' said his mother. 'Nan rushes upstairs without so much

51

as a nod in my direction, while you can't wait to get the whisky out. Something happened to upset you both. I don't like being left in the dark.'

Barry would have preferred to forget the whole incident, but he felt he owed her an explanation; on the other hand, he had no wish to alarm her unduly by a detailed description of what had happened.

'Some silly kids got a bit worked up. Didn't like the idea of their team losing, I suppose. When we came out they started smashing the car about, and trying to get at me. It wasn't much really.'

'Wasn't much, Barry! They were like wild animals. You should have seen them, Mum. They'd have killed us if they could,' said Nan.

'It's best to forget the whole thing. Anyway, the damage isn't much.'

His mother clucked: 'You know Barry, if crowds are going to get like this I don't think you should make Nan go to matches. It's not as if she liked it really.'

'He didn't *make* me, Mum. I wanted to go. Anyhow, it's only once in a blue moon.'

'No, Mum's right. It was selfish of me. But what annoys me more than anything is the unreasonableness of those kids. I've got nothing to rebuke myself over. I couldn't have been more impartial.'

His mother rose. 'Don't let's have an inquest. You both want to relax, have a meal, then a good night's sleep. And as for you, Barry, don't go tossing and turning all night worrying about it. You're supposed to enjoy it, not make yourself ill.'

Soon after 10 p.m. the two women went upstairs. Barry said, 'I'll be up in a jiff.'

He watched a few minutes of television and was pleased to hear an announcer giving details of Sunday's programmes, say that there would be a film of the match. He decided he would watch it, if only to satisfy himself that the kids were entirely at fault and he had no reason to reproach himself.

Chapter IX

Wykeham was still clammy with fear as he pushed open the iron gate, tip-toed down the flight of area steps leading to the basement flat where he lived, and lifted the sisal door mat to grope underneath for the front door key.

Even the backs of his hands were perspiring, for the journey home had been an absolute nightmare, and as he did not possess a watch he had lost all count of time.

When he jumped from the train he had reached the top of the embankment and found himself alone. From that moment he had been gripped in a fearful panic. Although he had not been guilty of any violence, and had even held back when the carriage was being wrecked, he knew he could never bring himself to deny it if stopped and questioned by a policeman. If Ben and the others ever got to hear he had saved his neck by washing his hands of their activities, he would never again be accepted in their company. He would rather lie than be the butt of their ridicule and contempt.

Meanwhile, his main problem had been to get home somehow or other. He had neither the courage nor the confidence of Ben, so could not bring himself to hitch a lift; instead, he had walked and run, walked and run, religiously adhering to a hundred steps of each as he had been taught as a boy scout, until he reached a roadside cafe, the car park of which was packed with massive lorries carrying tarpaulin-covered cargoes. Taking a gamble, he had clambered up the back of one and squeezed under a tarpaulin. It had seemed hours before the driver got into the cab, started the engine and swung on to the road.

The stench had been indescribable, and when his outstretched hand had touched hair on a stiff backing, he realised he was lying on a cargo of hides from an abbatoir. Whenever the lorry stopped at traffic lights, the hiss of the air brakes had petrified him. And all the time, he had anticipated the cover being lifted, a torch being shone into his eyes and a voice demanding, 'Hullo – what are you up to?' As time passed he had become bolder and peeped out, but he was unable to form any idea as to where he was, for all he could see were the backs of signposts, and those on the other side of the road were out of vision before he could read them. He lay shivering for what had seemed an eternity as the lorry thundered through the night. There was a stop, but just long enough for the driver to relieve himself, and when Wykeham lifted the tarpaulin he had seen a signpost indicating that London was seven miles away. Rather than risk going to an unwanted destination, he had jumped down and begun to walk.

Now he was home, and his fear if anything had increased, for his leisure life was unknown to his family. They would have been horrified, and felt compelled to seek immediate remedies to wean him away from the company he found so essential and desirable.

He lived with his mother and father in a flat-divided house that had been scheduled for demolition many years ago, but had been repeatedly reprieved because of the acute housing shortage in the area.

Wykeham turned the key and closed the door as silently as possible.

54

'That you?' he heard his father call.

'It's all right, Dad, go back to sleep.'

There was a click of a lamp switch and the room was suddenly illuminated, and Wykeham could see that his father had been sitting up in the armchair with his overcoat on top of his pyjamas.

'What you mean, boy – go back to sleep. I could not sleep.'

There was bewilderment in his voice. 'Just what time you call this? We been worried sick. No football games go on as long as this hour. We heard about all the troubles and worried in case you was hurt at all.'

His father was in his mid-fifties but looked older, and his crinkled hair was a slate grey colour. The room was hopelessly over-cluttered with solid furniture. Above the fireplace was a plaster crucifix, and on another wall was a framed sacred heart.

Wykeham sat on the edge of a chair and pulled off his boots, 'Look, Dad, I'm sorry. But I'm home now. I can't keep my eyes open. I'm going to bed.'

'No, son. No boy stops out that late and just goes to bed. I want to hear from you yourself, why you so late home.'

'There's no mystery, honest. I missed the train. Simple as that.'

'Listen, boy. Your mother and I were real sick with worry. We just don't want you to go around with no good people. Now you tell me that and we can all go to bed.' He had the soft lilting voice of the West Indian, which was ill-suited to anger, and nullified the urgency of his demands. The tiredness and prolonged fear were too much for Wykeham, and he suddenly lowered his head and began to cry like a small over-tired child. 'I haven't done anything, I tell you. So why keep on and on?'

'All right. Go to bed. But just let me tell you this, Wyke-

55

ham. We got a nice home here, and I got a good job ...
steady hours, five days a week, and no danger of short time.
Now, I don't want to lose that because you done something
without thinking. We're not outcasts here no more. It took a
long time for us to be all right with many people. Don't you
go spoil it by giving us a bad name.'

Wykeham was relieved when his father rose and made
for his own bedroom. The inquisition such as it had been
was over.

In the privacy of his room, Wykeham prayed fervently
and besought God to let him escape arrest or involvement
over the night's trouble. From his deep religious upbringing
he was aware that this was the wrong way to pray, and so he
interspersed his begging with promises that he would re-
form. But nagging at the back of his mind was the knowledge that he would never forsake Ben and his friends. He
would, however, try and act like a disciple in their midst,
and tactfully point out the error of their ways, and stress
how they could still have fun without aggro.

Chapter X

The only illumination in the curtain-drawn room came
from the bluish flicker of the television screen showing a
film of the match which had sent Ben's hopes crashing. He
was craning forward on the settee, his elbows resting on his
knees, his chin cupped in the palms of his hands, listening
intently to every word of the commentary. Almost uncon-
sciously he reached down for the beer between his feet,
drank noisily and deeply, but never took his eyes off the
screen. May sat to one side of the room attempting to darn

56

a pile of socks in the poor light. Occasionally she glanced at the screen, but more frequently looked towards the plateful of cut sandwiches on the coffee table and remarked, 'Come on, no one seems to be hungry.'

Henry sat in his own chair clutching a white china tankard. He made frequent interjections to express derision, contempt and outright indignation, but nobody paid any attention.

Jeannie was sitting beside Ben, but she was not hearing a word of the commentary, and although her eyes were focused on the screen she was not really taking in what she was seeing; for her thoughts were with her father, and the words running through her head were those that had followed the announcement that she was going round to Ben's house. He had made a mild protest in his long-suffering voice, a voice that never seemed to take on a different note these days, and his stock phrases spluttered out, 'I'm only interested in what's good for *you*. You're all I've got now, remember.' It was the way he said it that made Jeannie feel she was being held a captive replacement for her dead mother. When first he had become attentive and over-anxious about her future, she had been flattered, but gradually the over-possessiveness and veiled threats had begun to sour her, and his awful suffocating kindness grated.

The monotonous reminders of, 'You're so much like your mother,' and the constant assurances that she was worth all the sacrifices he made, had alienated her affections. It made her realise how lucky she was in having Ben. No wheedling from him. Not a hope of that, thank God. Ben was dominant and that's how a girl wanted it. Tell *you* what to do, with no bones about it. If only her father would put his foot down once in a while, instead of forbidding her to do something, then immediately capitulating and giving her his blessing. Cunningly, she now used his doting to her own

57

advantage, for she knew that no matter how much he might object to something, he would end up agreeing with her, because she could twist him round her little finger. And this alone made her feel contemptuous of him.

As the television glowed, the only picture she saw was the scene a couple of hours earlier when she had got ready to meet Ben. She had been unable to define it, but the thought of actually going to his house had stirred her and aroused something that she could only accept as being a bit sloppy.

In deference to the occasion she had put on a short mini skirt with a belt and large brass buckle that nestled just on her navel, a white frilly-fronted blouse, a new pair of panti-tights, and her best pair of shoes – squat, square-heeled, glistening plastic.

Dad had stood in the doorway leaning against the jamb. 'Going out?' he asked in a voice that intimated betrayal.

'Yes, Dad. Round to Ben's house.'

'Your hair looks lovely. Like your mother's. Only she wore it a bit longer. I must say that get-up suits you. You *can* look like a girl when you want to.'

And so it had gone on, even to the extent of helping her on with her coat and fussing in the way that annoyed her beyond words.

'I don't suppose it would be any good asking you not to go round? I don't want you to get too wrapped up. I'm only thinking of *you*. Your mother, now, had a good look round before settling steady with me. That's the right and proper way to go about it.'

Finally, her temper had flared and he had given up his protests, and turned them into honeyed words of full approval.

The reverie passed, and she was physically aware of Ben beside her. She moved her leg until it was pressing against

58

his thigh; then, encouraged by the darkness, she slid her hand along until it rested on his knee. She felt his leg jerk in acknowledgement, and although he did not move his cupped hands from his face, she realised it was a gesture of approval. Briskly, like a salute, his right hand moved from his face and held hers. 'This is it, just coming up. You'll see how right we were.'

The commentator was saying: 'Now we come to those vital seconds that decided the match. Number nine is going through with an open goal in front when he is up-ended. Unhesitatingly, referee Hudson points to the spot and awards a penalty.'

In a few seconds the incident was over, the penalty was taken, and the disconsolate goal-keeper was seen kicking the ball upfield.

The commentator said, 'We'll watch that again in slow motion and see whether Mr Hudson's snap decision was the right one.'

The television screen showed the footballers moving with ghostly slowness as the centre-forward was sent into the air, curling slowly like a floating feather until he hit the ground. The referee's hand as it pointed to the spot was so slow-moving that it gave the impression that he had all the time in the world to make his decision.

The commentator intruded again: 'As you can see, it was a perfectly fair tackle, and if Mr Hudson, who hails from Boxley, is watching, I'm sure he'd be the first to agree. But that's not the point. The ref's word is final, and any player will accept that. Wrong decisions are the rub of the green.'

Ben rose and switched off the set, then turned and addressed everyone in general. 'What did I tell you? He was bent. Bent as a bloody corkscrew. Come on, Jeannie, let's go to the disco. I can't stand any more of that crap.'

59

She rose obediently. May protested, 'But you haven't eaten all the sandwiches. Do you have to dash off? Anyway, it's not over yet.'

'We've seen what we want, Mum.'

May capitulated, dry-washed her hands, and said, 'Nice to have you round, dear. Jeannie, isn't it?' Acknowledging the nod of confirmation with a smile, May went on, 'Do pop round again. It's nice to see Little Ben settling down. I hope we'll be seeing quite a lot of you from now on.'

Jeannie turned to Ben, her eyes begging approval. 'It's up to him really.'

Henry rose and gave her a two-handed handshake that was exaggeratedly fervent. 'Pretty little thing like you should take his mind off football.'

May shushed him with a shocked, 'Henry!'

'Only kidding,' he hastily assured her, and then to impress everyone he had meant no offence, went off at a tangent. 'Pity about that foul...'

'It was a fair tackle. You want to get a pair of National Health specs,' Ben snorted.

May sensed a row brewing and quickly intervened. 'Get Jeannie's coat, Little Ben. Then off you go and enjoy yourselves. No point in being cooped up indoors when it's nice outside.'

Ben went into the passage and collected the coat from the wall rack and handed it to Jeannie. 'Well, help her on with it. There's a dear,' said May.

He did, but grudgingly, pointing out, 'I'm not a cloakroom attendant, Mum.'

'Manners never hurt anyone. Now run along.'

In the lift, Ben fixed his eyes on the floor indicator, watching the small green numbers light up as they descended, as if willing it to go faster. Jeannie leaned against the wall and studied his face until the intensity of her stare must have communicated itself to Ben, for he turned and demanded, 'What you goggling at me for? Like what you see?'

'Yes, a lot. Would you like to kiss me, Ben?'

'Not partic.'

'Oh,' she said, deflated.

'All right, but you know I don't go much on all that sloppy stuff.'

They were still kissing when the lift reached the ground floor and the automatic doors opened. A man and his wife were waiting to get in.

'Break it up, mate,' said the man. 'Keep your courting for the park.' Ben gave him a two-fingered sign, but he was smiling.

They walked hand in hand towards the padlocked motor scooter and Ben said, 'Hope you weren't too bored upstairs.'

'No, I loved it. Really. I hope you ask me again.'

'Yes, but let's wait till one night when the old man's out. He really gets me the way he rabbits on.'

When the scooter was unpadlocked, Jeannie straddled the pillion seat and hung on grimly as Ben raced recklessly to the disco. Their hearts were still pounding from the moments shared in the lift, and in some indefinable way they knew their association had altered.

Chapter XI

The discotheque was so jam-packed that as they walked down the steep stairs, they felt the body heat hit them as if an oven door had been opened, while the accumulated stale-fresh tobacco smoke made their eyes smart.

Once their eyes had become accustomed to the gloom, they could see several of the gang were already there, some lounging in rubber-boned positions, while others were dancing, eyes diverted, with arms working like heel and toe walkers. Ben shouldered his way through the dancers, with Jeannie following close behind in the path he had forced. He sat down behind a table at the far end of the room. Immediately he was surrounded by the gang, whose faces he could hardly see as flickering candles jammed in bottle tops were the sole source of light.

'Any of you see the telly?' It was more an order than an enquiry. There were several nods of assent; others more loquacious made remarks such as, 'A diabolical liberty,' and, 'Bugger should be blacklisted,' or, 'I know where I'd like to have stuck that football.'

'Well, it proved what I've said all along,' said Ben. 'Personally I don't think we should let him get away with it.' It was a direct demand for action.

They all agreed with his sentiments, but as one put it, 'What can *we* do about it?'

'I'll think up something, don't worry. And when I do, we'll get cracking on it, pronto.'

There was a painful studied silence when Caleb came in and perched on the corner of the table. As no one spoke, he was eventually forced to say, 'Hi, Ben. Hi, gang,' to draw attention to his presence.

'Get off my table, and bugger off. I'm surprised you got the neck to come in here at all,' said Ben.

'What have I done?'

'Nothing, just nothing. That's why you can shove off.' Ben stabbed at him with a forefinger, and spelled out each word slowly. 'You are chicken. You backed down every time. First it was outside the ground, then in the coach. Yet in you bowl, bold as brass, as if nothing had happened. Well, Caleb, there's no room in our set-up for you. So piss off. And don't think that's just my view. The others all go along with me.'

A chorus of agreement greeted his remarks, and the coloured youth felt a sick tightening in his stomach as he realised he was being banished. 'Ben, it won't happen again. I promise. God's honour. Please let me stay.'

'No dice. You say that every time, yet when the crunch comes your bottle goes. Truth is, you cotton pickers are all wind and piss. You can't stand the thought of not being under-privileged. You just got to be nice to everyone. Anyway, we got something lined up, and who's to know you wouldn't squeal if someone leant on you.'

The coloured boy crossed his heart and drew a forefinger across his throat. 'I swear on my life, Ben. I wouldn't. Honest. Look, you and me see eye to eye now. We didn't before. But I've sorted that out with myself, Ben. You don't have to go worrying on that score.'

The brash, brazen words, clashed with his secret thoughts which were turned heavenwards and seeking forgiveness for betraying his earlier prayers.

'Just talk again, Caleb. You certainly are good when it comes to the word stakes.'

'Ben, you try me. Go on. Just try me and see.'

Ben was so flattered at the power he exerted over Caleb, he decided it would be arrant foolishness to expel him from the company, for where else would he find such a perfect symbol of his authority.

'It's up to the lads, really. I'm quite happy myself to give you another chance,' he said nonchalantly, and canvassed the group with his eyes.

Immediately they realised Ben was *telling* them what to do not asking them. Nevertheless, they hummed and hawed before unanimously agreeing that Caleb should be given one more chance.

The gratitude for a reprieve was apparent in Caleb's sob-repressed voice. 'You won't regret this. You really won't. And I mean that.'

'All right. We'll take a chance. You other kids slide off while we talk business.'

Ben's dictate was readily obeyed, and they moved from the table to the dance square.

'You'll go the whole hog?'

'Ben, I've given my word, haven't I?'

'Yes, but I'm not sure how much it's worth. Tell me, what's your job?'

'Post Office.'

'I know that, thick head. But doing what? I don't expect you stand on the street corner with your mouth open waiting for people to pop letters in, now do I?'

Over-anxious to please, Caleb explained, in tedious detail, that he worked in the sorting section.

'If I told you a bloke's name and the town he lived in, could you get an address on a Sunday?' Ben asked in a conspiratorial whisper.

'We never close. If he's on the phone, quicker than that,' said the coloured boy, snapping his thumb and forefinger. 'We got a stack of phone books that cover the whole land. Why do you want it?'

'You and me are going to see him, that's why.'

He took a scrap of paper from his pocket and wrote on it, then slipped it across the table. 'That's his name, and that's the town, and don't you breathe a word to anyone, or I'll have your guts for garters. And I kid you not, Caleb.'

In his anxiety to please, Caleb said, 'Tell you what, Ben. I'll do it now. You sit there twenty minutes and I'll be back. How's that for service?'

It was actually twenty-five minutes later when he returned, and with a flourish of triumph handed Ben a slip of paper with Hudson's full address on it.

'Bloody good work, Caleb. That's what I call efficiency.'

Caleb didn't admit how easy it had been. He shrugged, 'Anything for the boss.'

In truth it had been simple. He had ridden his scooter to his work and gone to the files of telephone directories.

'What brings you in?' the foreman had asked, but that had presented no problem. 'Got to look up a number of a friend,' he had lied.

'It must be important, that's all I can say, if it couldn't wait till morning. Wild horses wouldn't drag me in here on a Sunday if I was off.'

It had taken him less than three minutes to find the address as there were only a few Hudsons in the book, and only one in Boxley, and he had ringed it with his ball-point pen while he went away to get a sheet of paper on which to copy the details. The foreman had enquired kindly, 'Hope it isn't bad news son – wanting it in such a hurry, I mean.'

Ben tucked it away in his pocket. 'Meet me down here after work tomorrow. With your scooter. We're going to pay Mr bloody-bent-Hudson a visit. And don't you mention it to no one.'

'You can count on me, Ben. Anything you can do – as the saying goes,' he said. Secretly he wasn't unduly alarmed. The referee bloke was pretty untouchable. You had only to see the way the fuzz rushed to his help to realise that. But it would prove that he was prepared to go along with Ben.

Chapter XII

The orange globe of the Belisha beacon outside Hudson's
house blinked on and off with the monotonous regularity of
a pulse beat, first illuminating, then darkening the front
door. Ben stood behind the broad, concealing trunk of a
roadside horsechestnut and took stock of the situation,
while Caleb and Jeannie furtively wheeled the scooters
along a narrow gravel path leading to what appeared to be a
public open space, for there were hard-surfaced tennis
courts with high wire netting, a manicured bowling green, a
concrete cricket strip and the shadowy shapes of goal-posts
at the end of mud-churned pitches. When they had rested
them, out of sight, against the wall of a neglected timber-
walled pavilion, they rejoined him in the shadows. Ben was
tugging his lower lip with pincered fingers, as if the tweak-
ing was an essential aid to concentration. His pulse was
racing with the anticipation of what was to come.

'That Belisha's a bit of a sod. They can see anyone who
gets within ten yards of that house.' His words invited a
reply.

Caleb, with a swallowy nervousness, said, 'I'm with you
all the way, Ben. Just put me in the picture that's all. I'm
entitled to that.' The fear in his voice was so evident that he
might just as well have openly pleaded for the abandon-
ment of whatever they were supposed to be doing. But as he
was still undecided about his purpose, Ben assumed an
arrogant, authoritative air, and snapped, 'That's just what I
feared from you, Caleb, chickening out. We no sooner get
here than you get an attack of the squitters. Jesus, you bind

66

me rigid.'

In the enveloping dark he could barely see the coloured boy, who somehow or other had managed to transmit his fear, and this acted as a calming balm to Ben's own jitteriness, and served to make him sound as if he was in full control of the situation. 'We'll have to do that light.'

'I'll do it,' volunteered Caleb.

'How?' enquired Ben derisively.

'With a stone. I guarantee to hit it first time,' he boasted.

'And wake the whole neighbourhood in the bargain! Anyway, it's too risky, you might cock it up and miss.'

'I never miss, Ben. I'll bet you a pound to a penny.'

Jeannie groped around in the dark at the base of the tree; when she straightened up she had an egg-sized stone in her hand. 'Here, Caleb. Put your money where your mouth is. I've got ten pence that says you'll miss.'

Caleb took the stone and weighed it carefully in his right hand before extending his arm like a dart thrower and lobbing it in a slow parabola towards the beacon. The tinkle of broken glass followed, and simultaneously the light went out. They waited quietly in the dark, and seconds later the front porch of Hudson's home glowed brightly as the door opened, silhouetting a man and a woman. The woman's voice said, 'What on earth caused that?'

They heard the man reply indifferently, 'Stone from a car I expect.'

The woman insisted, 'But I didn't hear anything.'

'Let's face it, we haven't been sitting with our ears glued to the window waiting to hear passing cars. Anyway, don't look a gift horse in the mouth. It's always been a darned nuisance.'

The porch was again encased in darkness as the door closed behind them.

'Bloody good shot, Caleb,' said Ben. 'At least we know they're in.'

'Here,' whispered Jeannie. 'Take it.'

'What?' asked Caleb.

'The bloody ten pence, you nit. You won it, so take it.'

The money changed hands and they stood silently in the shadow of the tree listening to their own breathing, until Jeannie asked, 'What's the next move, Ben?'

'I'm thinking. We got to get him out somehow.'

'What about the phone?' suggested Caleb.

'Oh, brilliant. And what do we say? Please come out so we can duff you up? He'll do that on the double for sure. No, we got to think of something else.'

For two or three minutes they discussed with lowered voices the possible ruses to lure him out, but none of them were practical. They were saved further thought when the porch was illuminated again. Seconds later they saw the same two shapes, close-linked in an embrace.

Hudson said, 'Won't be long, darling. A couple of times round the common, then straight back. Just enough to get the blood moving.'

The woman's reply was inaudible, but they saw the man come down the path and break into a jog trot, taking deep noisy breaths like a boxer.

'Christ, he's going for a run,' Ben whispered. 'He's even got a track-suit on. We're in luck all right.'

As Hudson set off along the pavement, they could hear the cushioned plop of his plimsolled feet. 'O.K. let's go,' said Jeannie.

'Don't rush it. Let him get up the road first. We don't want his old woman dashing out in a panic,' warned Ben.

Jeannie was once more on her hands and knees groping on the ground, prompting Ben to ask harshly, 'What the hell you looking for?'

68

'A big rock. Caleb can have a coconut shy at his nut if he's that good.'

Ben's disgusted snort was an ample expression of what he thought of the idea, and in place of words he grabbed her arm and tugged her in the direction of the disappearing referee. Caleb followed with lagging steps that fully expressed his lack of enthusiasm for the venture. Cautiously, they kept a discreet distance behind the runner, but the safety precautions seemed totally unnecessary as Hudson was completely engrossed in his exercise, and still emitting the deep snorts, now punctuated with grunts of, 'In – out, in – out, as if stroking a boat's crew. Suddenly the plop of his feet on the pavement gave way to the whisper of shifting gravel.

'He's going in where we left the scooters,' whispered Jeannie.

'Good for us,' said Ben. 'We'll have him on our own.'

'What we going to do?' asked Caleb uncertainly.

'How the fuck do I know. We'll just have to play it by ear,' snapped Ben, as they turned down the gravel path and saw the figure of Hudson heading round the perimeter of the open space at a much quickened pace. The three of them were now panting heavily, while Ben and Jeannie were riddled with indignation that the referee had out-paced them and left them with little or no chance of catching him up. Caleb was secretly relieved and hoped he would run even faster.

'Get the scooters,' snapped Ben.

The silence was suddenly broken by the staccato pop-pop of the engines. Jeannie swung up behind Ben and he raced the scooter at full throttle across the bumpy grass, with Caleb following less than two feet behind. Hudson swung round in alarm as the machines neared him, and stopped in his tracks to demand, 'What the hell does this mean?'

Ben swung the scooter to within a few inches of him, then lashed out viciously with his right boot. The blow caught Hudson on the fleshy part of his thigh and he grunted in pain. 'Take him, Caleb,' shouted Ben, as he turned the scooter in a wide sweep and headed for the motionless, petrified man once more. Caleb came in fast but made no attempt to kick Hudson who aimed a wild swipe at the mounted figure, but completely missed him.

'This is ridiculous. What's going on?' shouted Hudson, the fear tangible in his voice. Ben swung the scooter round again, his right boot churning up the ground like a dirt track rider, and drove straight at him again. This time Jeannie thrust out a foot that caught him in the back of the knee and sent him crashing to the ground. 'You're not here for the fucking ride, Caleb. Put the boot in, you windy sod.'

On hearing the rebuke, Caleb gave the scooter full throttle and headed for the prostrate figure, aiming a half-hearted kick that he hoped would miss. But the impact of his foot against the body of the man on the floor was so solid it almost threw him off his scooter, and he wobbled erratically before bringing it back under control.

Hudson somehow managed to regain his feet and began to limp towards the entrance, clutching his side. Ben screamed hysterically, 'Put your headlights on. We'll blind the bastard. Cut him off.'

Instantly the darkness was pierced by the undipped beams of several headlights. The sudden glare brought Hudson to a stop as the lights hit him fully in the eyes, and he stood immobile trying to shield his eyes with cupped hands, and turning his head from side to side. The two scooters began harrying him like whippets after a mesmerised hare. Each time they raced in they aimed blows some of which missed, while others struck home with sickening crunches. Hudson stood his ground, swiping wildly and as ineffectively as a man tormented by hornets. His fear mounted. The blows from the hard-capped boots were rapidly sapping his energy, while the blinding lights obscured his targets as they came straight at him in a deafening roar. Once a front guard struck him a glancing chest blow that set the scooter careering crazily across the grass, but the rider dextrously regained control and came in again. After one desperate lunge, Hudson recoiled in horror as his hands grasped something furry. As he dropped it, he realised it was one of the emblems that youngsters trailed behind their mopeds.

'Get off and fight like men,' he appealed, only to grunt in pain as a scooter passed within inches and a needle-sharp pain shot from his broken knee cap to the top of his leg. He fell to the ground writhing in agony. The pain seemed to be shooting through all parts of his body. Raising himself on an elbow he yelled as loudly as possible, 'Help – help – help.' But he got no more words out before he felt the crunch of a boot strike him in the mouth, which was suddenly filled with the salty taste of blood. He spat out two teeth, and gave up the unequal struggle and lay on the ground panting and sobbing in pain and frustration. Suddenly all was mercifully quiet. There was no longer the intimidating roar of engines, followed by the thud of boots against his body. They have gone, he thought. He struggled painfully to his feet and realised his error. Coming towards him were three shadowy, menacing figures; behind them were the scooters, balanced on their parking rests, their lights now out. The faces were just a blur, but he could make out that one was much bigger than the others, while one seemed a mere slip of a boy. All the orders seemed to be coming from the big one. As they neared him he clenched his fist and took up the challenging pose of a boxer. He realised what a forlorn gesture it was, because nothing would stop them now. At the same time, he managed to think how ridiculous it was that no one seemed to have heard the awful commotion. His ingrained sense of fair play made him feel they would listen to reason.

'Look, let's be reasonable. If I've done something, let's sort it out.' Then the thought crossed his mind that perhaps they were out to rob him. 'If it's money you want, you're wasting your time. I've nothing on me.' And he realised rather stupidly that he was tugging at his track-suit to indicate that he had no pockets.

The big one and the small one pounced like jackals on a dying prey. A flame of agony shot through his groin, followed by a head butting him fully on the bridge of his nose. Blows seemed to come from everywhere. The smallest of the three was on the ground grabbing his leg. He tried to shake it clear, and then he felt the searing pain of teeth being sunk into his leg. He lost count of the kicks as he lay on the ground whimpering. He could hear his own voice like an injured animal, and felt vaguely ashamed that he had not routed them. Pain, acute as a burn, shot through his head as an ear-drum ruptured. He was grateful that one of the trio seemed to be holding back.

Hudson lay motionless, his head cradled on his forearm, taking the kicks unfeelingly. He could hear the impact, but there was no longer any pain.

'Come on. The bastard's been taught his lesson.' He recognised the voice of the big one. 'He'll know he's been in a punch-up in the morning.'

'Give him one for luck, Caleb.'

'No, Jeannie. He's hurt bad.'

For the first time Hudson realised one of the three was a girl, but he was past caring. The earth was close to his nostrils and he could smell the turf.

His head jerked as Ben's boot hit him behind the ear.

72

The scooters started, raced, and he heard them fade in the distance. Hudson made no attempt to rise. He was tired, desperately tired. He would sleep a little while.

Hudson died without even the consolation of knowing why.

Nan woke and automatically reached across the bed for the comforting bulk of her husband. She patted the vacant space several times before realising he was not there. Her hand groped overhead for the tassel of the light switch, and for the first time panic flooded through her as she took in the empty space, then the face of the bedside alarm clock. It was nearly midnight. Softly, so as not to wake the children, she called out his name. Then repeated it louder when there was no response. Her feet shuffled into her slippers and she put on her dressing gown and tiptoed downstairs, hoping to find him asleep in the armchair. It had happened before, she told herself, so there really was no need for this sense of foreboding. But the chair was empty.

Nan took the rubber-cased torch from the hook in the kitchen and ran to the corner, her heels clopping on the pavement. She realised that something dreadful had occurred.

She swept the turf with the torch beam, and it was only a matter of seconds before the crumpled form was spotlighted. As she knelt beside it, the amount of blood was enough to tell her that Barry had been the victim of a brutal assault. She shook him gently and called his name, felt for a pulse beat, found none, then listened, head on his chest, for the reassuring sound of his heart. It was silent.

Back home she calmly sat on the telephone stool in the hall and dialled 999. It burred briefly before the operator brusquely asked, 'Fire, ambulance or police?'

'Police, please. I wish to report a murder.' Ultra-cautious over hoax calls, the operator insisted on a telephone number before putting her through.

Chapter XIII

Detective Chief Superintendent Cyril Porter removed his dinner jacket and draped it carefully over the back of a chair, smoothing out the creases as he did so; then he went to the refrigerator and poured a tumbler of ice cold milk which he placed on a glass mat on the table beside his single divan bed. Returning to the kitchen he filled another glass with water and dropped in two Alka Seltzer tablets, and watched them bubble and bounce on the bottom of the glass.

Porter was a heavily built man in his late forties, with a fine head of near-white hair and the first intimations of a jowl. His actions, even when pottering around his flat, had an air of authority and calculated method. Not surprisingly, he tackled his job in the same way, and he was grateful for the training that had instilled in him the paramount importance of routine, rather than the inspirational flare so beloved by writers of detective fiction. Having been mainly concerned with murder for many years, he knew you got the best results by making detectives leg it from house to house with questionnaires that were checked, cross-checked and further checked for that vital discrepancy. And he knew the value of finger-printing all the men in a village, and blood sampling them too. Slow it might be, but it was quicker in the long run than sticking your backside in a Parker Knoll and playing the violin while you waited for the divine revelation.

Porter had moved into the flat two years ago when his wife died. He had chosen it because it was only two miles from his office.

The tablets had dissolved, leaving a white coating round the rim of the glass. He drank it down in a long swallow and reflected that it had been a pleasant evening, although the drinking had been a bit on the ferocious side. A friend had invited him as a guest to the National Sporting Club for an evening of boxing, eating and boozing, and he had enjoyed it immensely, for there was a tendency these days, being on his own, to spend too much time on the job and not enough on relaxing.

The phone rang and he walked through to the bedroom to pick up the receiver. His left hand pushed a note pad into position. 'Porter,' was all he said.

'Morning, guvnor. Hope I didn't get you out of bed.'

'I know how the thought of upsetting my sleep would worry you sick, George. But get on with it. What's on, laddie?'

The voice at the other end belonged to Detective Sergeant George Rowan, a young officer who Porter was convinced was destined for a brilliant career, having all the attributes of a good copper: a sense of vocation, a quick mind and the ability to slog on when it all seemed pointless.

'We seem to have a big one, sir. Man called Hudson battered to death on the common. Wife found him, but she couldn't possibly have done it. Too bloody savage by half. I've been there, but only had a cursory look. Called you right away.'

'George, you'll have to send down one of the patrol cars for me. I've been on the sherbert with some pals, and I won't risk driving myself if there are any of those uniformed lads around. They'd love nothing better than to breathalyse me. And George, I don't want anyone trampling around the scene. Also get a photographer and the pathologist. See if Professor Render is on tap. And rope the whole bloody area off if necessary.'

Porter issued a few more instructions, went into the bedroom and drank the milk, slipped on his dinner jacket, put on a top coat, filled his cigarette case, then went down to the front hall to await the arrival of the police car.

From experience, Porter knew it took him approximately eight minutes to smoke a cigarette, and he was only half way through it before the black squad car pulled up outside. The driver really must have put his foot down.

'Morning, sir. Not very nice to be dragged out at this hour.'

'I don't mind. It's not being dragged out that annoys me. I like to get to the scene quickly before half the force has trampled the evidence into insignificance with their bloody great issue boots.'

When they reached the entrance to the common, a crowd of people with heavy overcoats over their night attire was being held back by a uniformed policeman who was insisting quite unconvincingly, 'There's nothing for you to see. So you might as well all go back to bed again.'

'Shall I go straight through, sir?' asked the driver.

'No, drop me here. I don't want the car churning things up. Somewhere out there is something that'll give us the answer to this little howdyoudo. Whether we find it or not is a different matter. But take my word, laddie, it's there.'

Sergeant Rowan emerged from the shadows and opened the car door. 'Bit like one of those old English movies, sir.'

'What on earth are you rabbiting on about, George?'

'The toff detective. Turning up in dinner jacket to sort it all out. Lord Peter Wimsey and all that.' He circled an eye

76

with two fingers like a monocle.

'George, I think you are wasted in this job. You ought to be on television. Now take me to it, and let's hear what you know.'

In the distance, a circle of arc lights had been erected, and were directed at a dark indistinguishable shape on the ground. As the two men walked towards it, Rowan outlined the steps he had taken. Mrs Hudson's doctor had seen her, and although she was in a state of shock she was capable of being interviewed. A van-load of police officers had been called in, but he had not got them searching until he had Porter's opinion.

'No, leave the search till first light. They can see what they're doing then. Rushing things in the dark often does more harm than good. There's not an awful lot we can do. But we'll see the wife in a minute. Maybe she knows the score.'

A police car had gone to pick up the pathologist who should be arriving any minute, said the sergeant. No, he hadn't been at all annoyed at being called out. Like you, he said he preferred to come when everything was nice and fresh. 'Made the point that it would be no more than a cursory examination. Time of death and so on.'

The two men stood gazing down at the body of Hudson which lay curled like a massive foetus. Much of the blood had congealed, and the face was almost unrecognisable. It was lacerated with deep cuts, the lips and eyes were blackened and swollen. One leg splayed out at an abnormal angle. White stakes had been driven into the ground and linked with white tape to record a rough outline of the murder scene.

'Jesus Christ! What they hit him with – a bulldozer, George?'

'They certainly did a thorough job, sir.'

'The track-suit mean anything, George?'

'Well I haven't had much time to do a lot, but it appears he was a top football referee and he had a fad about keeping fit. Ran round here every night according to his wife. I got that from the woman P.C. I put in with her. But you can chat her up yourself, sir.'

'All right, George. Now get some screens put up round the poor devil. Maybe the crowd at the gate will bugger off then.'

As they were talking, the pathologist arrived: a man with a high-domed head and a world-wide reputation for infallibility if not fairness.

'Morning, Superintendent. Morning, Sergeant. Taken all the pictures you need?'

Receiving an assurance that they had, he said. 'I'll have to disarrange the clothing a little to get a temperature. Sorry about that.'

The two men averted their eyes as the dead man was subjected to the indignity of a thermometer being inserted anally. They returned their gaze as he meticulously took temperature samples from the ground near the body.

Straightening up with a grunt that indicated that even his eminence could not ward off rheumatism, he brushed his trouser knees and remarked, 'Superintendent, I can't really help you a great deal. The time of death was around nine to ten p.m.'

Porter coughed discreetly. 'We can pin-point it a little closer I think, sir. His watch has been smashed. Stopped exactly at 9.46 p.m.'

A wry smile creased the pathologist's lips. 'I had noticed that, Superintendent. I was keeping it up my sleeve to en-hance my Papal aura.'

As he spoke, the pathologist made a rough pencil sketch on a pad, and added his first impressions of the scene, the injuries, the weather, type of soil and ground temperature.

78

'Check the ground temperature in an hour, please. And when the body's moved, wrap it in a polythene sheet. Put some plastic bags over his head and hands too. Then we'll be sure that nothing is lost or picked up in transit. His hands especially – what's under his nails should tell us what kind of struggle he put up, and who with.'

Then he peeled off his gloves and tucked them away in the black box of equipment he carried to all murder scenes. The gloves were not fastidiousness – extra fingerprints merely made more work for the police.

Putting an avuncular arm round the superintendent's shoulder, he began to lead him towards his car, talking as they walked. The informality of long years of working to-gether had established itself once the initial meeting, in which proper respect had been paid to their respective posi-tions, was over.

'Cyril, I'm not shoving off early. Frankly, I can serve no useful purpose here. Any one of several injuries could have killed him. Even a visual examination bears out massive brain damage. I'll do a full P.M. in the morning. Nine too late?'

'Not for me. I've still got a couple of hours work left here.'

Pausing by the wing of the police car, the pathologist fumbled in his overcoat pocket and produced a silver screw-top flask.

'As I'm being chauffered I can afford the indulgence.' After taking a long swig, he passed it to Porter. 'Return it in the morning. The flask I mean, not the contents.'

Porter strolled back to his sergeant, and behind the cover of a treetrunk they took long swallows of the warming spirit.

'Arrange for the body to be taken to the mortuary, George. The P.M. is at nine. I'd like you there. Now we'll see Mrs Hudson, and after that draw up what we want done first thing. We'll need a score of uniformed lads and a dozen C.I.D. Also see if the army engineers can rustle up a couple of mine detectors for us. They always oblige – the lads like the day out and their pictures in the papers.'

Porter sat in an armchair feeling ill at ease in his dinner jacket. He would have much preferred to keep his overcoat on, but Mrs Hudson had insisted on him removing it, and this was certainly no time to be self-conscious.

'I must apologise for my clothes,' he said weakly. 'I've been at a regimental reunion,' he lied. It seemed an inopportune moment to say he had been out enjoying himself.

'Please don't apologise, Mr Porter. You were not to know this awful thing would happen.'

Rowan was sitting inconspicuously on a hard-backed chair against the wall, a regulation note-book perched on his knee. His glance towards his superior confirmed that he too was thinking what a godsend it was that they didn't have a distraught woman on their hands, but one who was composed and in full command of her emotions.

'Would you like a cup of tea, gentlemen? Or perhaps something a little stronger? There is a little whisky left.'

Porter said, 'If it's not too much trouble, I'd love a whisky. I'm sure the sergeant would too.' He added the last part to let Rowan know he had no objection to his having a drink on duty. It was not as if they were going on a blind. But there was a more subtle motive behind his preference for a hard drink. Through countless films, books and television plays, the public had got the impression that policemen never sat down in other people's homes, and when offered a drink always retorted sternly, 'Not on duty, thank you,' which created a needlessly tense atmosphere, making even the innocent fear they were suspect. Porter liked people to relax, unless of course he was interrogating them, then there was no letting up. He liked to obtain their trust, then they confided and didn't skip the minor things for fear of antagonising, for it was the tit-bits that were so often important.

When the drinks had been poured, he began gently and coaxingly. 'First, is there anything we can do for you? Help with the children – transport to school? I suggest you let them go to school. With all the activity there's bound to be, it will only upset and confuse them. Keeping them at home would be a mistake.'

'No, thank you. My mother-in-law is coming over in the morning, and I do have transport.'

'Good. But if there is anything, please don't hesitate. I'm afraid there will be the question of a formal identification in the morning. Is there any relative you would prefer to do this for you?'

'No. I'll be all right. I did find him, remember. Nothing can shock me after that.'

He marvelled at her composure, but ruthlessly, because it was in her own interest, and would aid him in his duty, he pressed ahead with his questioning. Pushing much harder than normally he would have done, for there was always the possibility of a reaction setting in later, when he might be prevented from questioning her by some well-intentioned doctor.

At his request, she began at the beginning and recalled awakening in bed. 'I don't know why, but I just sensed something was wrong. I know it's silly, but that's how it was.'

'It's not silly, Mrs Hudson. I've encountered it many times in the past.'

She went back further, recalling the Belisha beacon, and he nodded for the sergeant to make a note of it. It could mean nothing or something.

Slowly and patiently he led her to a full recollection of the football match, and the ugly scene outside the ground after the game. The sergeant was busy writing, filling in page after page of his notebook in neat, almost child-like writing, which with years of practice he was able to do at a remarkable speed.

Nan accurately and without unnecessary elaboration described everything – the threats, the violence, the fear, the police inspector's timely intervention.

'Contact him in the morning for a full report, George.'

Nan ran dry, and said rather helplessly, 'That's all I'm afraid.'

'You've done wonderfully well, Mrs Hudson. Absolutely top rate. Just one thing, would you recognise any of them again?'

'I honestly doubt it. It was dark and they all looked so alike. Frankly, we were too concerned with getting away to take too much notice.' A long pause followed. 'There's one thing I recall. I hope it doesn't sound too ridiculous. There was a coloured boy ... shouting his head off outside the ground.'

'What did he shout? It may be important from an evidence point of view. Threats he intended to follow up?'

'I just don't know. I was crouched down most of the time.'

Rowan broke his silence. 'I very much doubt if he was peace-making. These coloured kids get very violent when roused.'

Porter rose. 'Let's leave it there for the time being, Mrs Hudson.'

As they walked to the waiting car, Porter remarked, 'What do you make of that, George?'

'Well, it seems the roots were at the match. But Christ knows what he could have done to deserve this.'

Nan Hudson went upstairs to see the children were tucked in and still alseep, then returned downstairs, where through

82

force of habit she took the chair opposite Barry's. It had suddenly turned chill. For warmth she wrapped a blanket around her shoulders, turned out all the lights and settled down to sleep. But Barry's presence was everywhere. The memories crowded back the more she tried to shut them out. She rested her head on her arm and wept quietly, for fear of waking the children. Finally, when exhaustion took over, she fell into a fitful doze, haunted by faces of screaming youths and the vision of his battered, mutilated face.

Chapter XIV

Porter sat in his drab office with his feet propped on top of a desk which was little more than an oblong slab of wood mounted on two tiers of drawers. Slowly and deliberately he rolled a cylindrical ebony ruler back and forth across the desk top as if it were a miniature steam roller flattening a stretch of newly tarred road.

He and the sergeant had just drawn up their plans for the enquiries to be made at sunrise. The first step had been the preparation of a long questionnaire which was now being run off on a duplicating machine. A team of fourteen detectives had been detailed to report early, and each would be given a pile of the forms and told to make house to house enquiries in the vicinity of the common. The form asked people where they had been during the vital hour before and after the murder, and the name and address of someone who could confirm their whereabouts. In time, these would be checked and cross-checked, so that those with legitimate explanations could be ruled out of the investigation, while further checks would be made on those which did not tie up. They would also be asked if they had heard or seen anything unusual, whether they knew the dead person, if they knew of any trouble in his life, and whether they would agree to be finger-printed. It was a stereotyped form which Porter had used many times in the past with varying degrees of success. He had a feeling that it would be useful in this case, for from what he had seen of the widow and the home, he was convinced there was no frustrated lover lurking in the background. And from the injuries inflicted he was certain that more than one person had attacked Hudson.

In addition to the team of detectives, fifty police constables had been told to report early for duty in suitable clothing, such as wellington boots, serviceable trousers, and thick jumpers. They would be required to carry out an inch by inch search of the ground, and to mark any discovery with a small wooden tag such as gardeners use to show the variety of seeds they have sown. On no account were they to touch anything.

Porter yawned and said, 'Well, that seems to have just about wrapped it up, George. Anything else occur to you that we ought to do?'

'Not really, guv. Frankly I could do with some shut-eye. No point in walking around in the morning like a wet dream fit for sweet Fanny Adams.'

'You won't be walking around. I want you at the P.M. I thought I'd mentioned it.'

'You did, but I was hoping you would have forgotten. Hate them myself.'

'George, I'd *pay* someone to take my place. I can't count how many I've been to, but I still feel like throwing up when I see someone being carved up like a side of beef. But you can't underrate their importance. Christ, it's the stench I can't stand.'

84

'There won't be much in this case, thank heavens. No time for decomposition.'

'There will be a different kind of stink if we don't pull somebody in pretty sharpish. A murder slap bang in the middle of a residential area! We'll have to pull out all stops on this one, George, or we'll have the guvnor breathing down our necks. And he can be a bloody old woman at times.'

At home, Cyril Porter carefully laid out a clean shirt, pair of socks, polished his shoes to a guardsman shine, set the alarm clock, poured a glass of milk – a sure preventive to ulcers – washed and got into bed. But he was unable to sleep, his mind was too active. Somewhere along the line this had something to do with football, which was a disconcerting thought as he knew literally nothing about the game which sent seemingly grown men crazy. He must remember in the morning to co-opt a young C.I.D. aide who knew something about football. Somebody who spent his spare time – if he was lucky enough to have any – standing on the terraces waving a rattle and yelling his head off. It might help to cut a few corners.

When a thought occurred to him he scribbled it down on his bedside pad. And it seemed to him he had hardly closed his eyes before the alarm clock was ringing.

Chapter XV

An hour after the post mortem, Porter was back in his office demanding to know what progress had been made.

One by one as the detectives on the house to house enquiries came in for a short break, Porter called them into his office. Nothing of any significance had been unearthed, and the main trouble seemed to be that when the murder was committed most of the local residents were glued to their television sets, and would not have heard a bomb go off, let alone a man scream. Further, many of the men folk were out at work and the officers would have to return later in the evening.

Even at this early stage Porter could sense that boredom was setting in among some of the younger officers, and he stressed upon them the importance of, 'sticking with it'. Later it might be necessary to read the riot act, but that time was a long way off yet. Young officers doing the dull routine legwork were never aware of the essential part their job played in an enquiry, and tended to become slap-dash and run the risk of overlooking a key factor. The same problem often arose with uniformed men detailed to search scrubland or woodland for a missing child; for a couple of days their sense of outrage made them tackle the job with enthusiasm, then as time passed they became lax, and a search disintegrated into a bush-prodding exercise, as if going through the motions was good enough.

Once the inevitable enamel jug of tea was delivered he sent for Wilcox, the young C.I.D. aide who he had been informed was a soccer fanatic. When the young constable walked diffidently into his room, Porter found it hard to disguise his sense of dismay as he waved the young man to a seat in an attempt to put him at ease. From his expression it was obvious he was expecting a ticking off and was wracking his memory to recall what could justify it.

'Relax, Wilcox. Have a cigarette. I don't suppose they bothered to tell you, but from now on you will be detached from all other duties to help me. I gather you are keen on football, lad?'

'Not to the detriment of the job, sir,' he hastened.

86

'Don't worry, this is to the advantage of it. May do you a bit of good when I submit my final report. If it ever gets to that stage.'

Wilcox sat twiddling with the cigarette realising he had no matches, and too overawed to ask for a light.

Porter leaned across the desk and flicked his lighter. 'I want you to gen up on the dead man. Antecedents. Find out all there is to know about him till you know him better than yourself. Check up on all his matches. Concentrate on any incidents that might have led to some aggro. Start now and go where you like. But don't overdo the expenses, lad. We're not made of money here.'

Wilcox was nodding his head in agreement at everything that was said, and Porter noticed that he was surreptitiously tapping the cigarette ash into the palm of his hand.

'There's an ash tray on the desk, lad. And a word of advice, on this job you'll have to be as bold as brass and bloody nosey, O.K.? And don't go around looking like a male model.'

For Porter was mildly surprised at the young aide's appearance: his hair was well below his ears although well groomed and brushed, while his suit with its lapelled waistcoat and crutch-hugging trousers, looked a trifle out of place on a young man who had decided to devote his life to crime detection and the apprehension of criminals. Porter, a firm believer in short back and sides, and the possessor of a coat-hangered row of charcoal grey suits and black pin-stripes, resignedly accepted this sartorial revolution as a sign of the times. At least no one would take Wilcox for a copper when he went around, and he was likely to find himself in some odd places.

'You'll be meeting some pretty down to earth characters, so play the part. Don't put them ill at ease with your appearance or approach. Dress neatly but inconspicuously.'

Fortunately, Wilcox looked incredibly youthful, which was a big advantage. Ruefully, Porter reminded himself of the old axiom that you were getting old when coppers looked young.

He said kindly, 'I think you'll do a good job, lad. Just keep in touch. And remember, don't rely on your memory. Write everything down in your book at the first convenient moment. Oh, and just one final thing. Keep your eyes and ears open for any chit-chat about a big coloured boy. And don't watch the clock – there'll be no clocking on and off for a while.'

Wilcox rose and rather surprisingly proferred his hand to Porter who, a trifle taken aback, shook it. 'Jesus,' he told himself. 'Roll on retirement. I'm getting out of my depth.'

When Wilcox left, Porter forced himself to catch up on his paper work. It was the unglamourous side of the job which the public never suspected existed. He pulled a wire-mesh tray towards him and attacked the pile of forms.

Once the reports were completed, he was free to get back to work again. He contacted Rowan on the intercom and announced he was returning to the scene of the crime.

A mobile canteen had been parked in one corner of the field, and a uniformed inspector was ready to give a run down on what had so far been revealed in the yard by yard search.

'There's one interesting find. Maybe the Zoo can help. One of the lads found what appears to be a fox's tail, or brush as the hunting fraternity call it, I believe,' said the inspector as he led them across the grass to where a tent-peg sized piece of wood marked the find. Attached to it was a buff luggage label.

'Haven't heard of a fox foraging around here,' said Porter flippantly, yet secretly pleased that something had been found. 'Get it down to the forensic boys. I'll bet you a pound to a pinch there hasn't been a fox around here since they last sighted a sabre-toothed tiger.'

An inch thick rope threaded through eyed iron-uprights encircled the area, and behind it was lined a large crowd of sightseers: women with prams and bawling babies, men with dogs, arm-in-arm couples, amateur photographers with still and cine cameras, and a bunch of kids obviously playing traunt.

The inspector continued talking as they stepped gingerly to another staked out spot. 'Even I know what this little lot is – smashed headlight. Car or motor cycle, though, I wouldn't know. There's also some odd skid marks and tyre impressions, which I should think are too disfigured to plaster cast. The ground's been well and truly churned up by football studs. Apart from that, nothing.'

Porter, hands in pockets, remarked, 'It's more than I hoped for. Have it all photographed and sent off with the other stuff.'

Several hours later, Porter and Rowan were in the police station waiting impatiently for a phone call from the forensic laboratory. It came quicker than they had anticipated. A voice said, 'I've got a surprise for you, sir. Your little fox tail is made of nylon. No self-respecting dog would even give it a sniff. As for the broken glass, I'm pretty certain it came from one of those scooter things that kids belt around on these days. I've practically pieced it together. Give us a bit more time and maybe we'll let you have some more information. Maker's name, period, etcetera. That help?'

'It certainly does,' said Porter. 'Thanks a lot. Cheers.'

He hung up and said to Rowan, 'I feel we're getting some place. Don't ask me where, but it's beginning to gell.'

It was 2 a.m. and Porter was alone. Being his own boss, he

had no one to telephone and ask if it was all right to knock off. So he sat alone in his office scanning through the last batch of questionnaires that had been dumped on his desk by the detective team going off duty. None of them revealed anything of the slightest importance, apart from one man who, while taking his dog 'to do his business' before being shut up for the night, did recall seeing a youth throw a stone at a Belisha beacon. But it was so dark, to put it in his own words, 'It would have been like trying to pick out a nigger in a coal mine.'

Another man had heard what could have been a scream or a shout, which he had ignored. The time? He hadn't bothered to look. His philosophy in life was simple – 'I don't poke my nose into anything that doesn't concern me. We keep ourselves very much to ourselves. Couldn't tell you my neighbour's name if you offered me a thousand.'

Porter tapped the forms neatly into order, placed them on the top of his desk and anchored them down with a paperweight.

As he put on his coat and hat he thought to himself, 'Jesus, I'll need some luck on this one, that's for sure.' But he quickly shrugged off his despondency. He had faced similar situations many times before. A murder hunt was the same as climbing a mountain – there was no short cut. You got there step by painful step.

Overtired, his brain overactive, he decided to walk home. It struck him that the smashed Belisha beacon might have a significance that he had overlooked. It was odd the man should have mentioned a coloured person, even if only metaphorically. He mulled over every conceivable possibility until he reached his flat.

When he opened the door the emptiness filled him with a sense of desolation, and though not an easily moved man he could appreciate the deadly sense of loss that pervaded the

Hudson home. This turned him to thinking of his quarry. As he took his milk into the bedroom, prepared his clothes for the morning, and set the alarm for six o'clock, he tried to draw a mental picture of the man he was seeking. What did he look like? What made him tick? What was he doing now? Was he holed up quivering in fear? Or was he completely indifferent to his act and cutting a bold figure by going about his work as if nothing had happened? Did he watch television or read the newspapers? Was he gradually disintegrating as the enormity of his crime became apparent? Or was he a hard case who didn't give a damn, and turned the knob or page to something more congenial?

Finally, he fell into a sleep that consisted of a jumbled, tumbled, out-of-sequence recollection of the day's work.

Chapter XVI

Ben was reading the newspaper over breakfast after a night of untroubled sleep. It was propped precariously against the cosied teapot and the marmalade jar, with the sports page facing him. He was so engrossed that he was totally unaware of what he was eating. Breakfast had been left by his mother who had gone out early, having been given the opportunity of earning some extra money by cleaning out the workshop of a local tailor. He was immersed in an article by a prominent football writer which analysed the decline, and forecast the fall of the Rovers. The criticism so enraged him that he promised himself that if he ever met up with the writer, he would give him a fourpenny one right between the fucking eyes.

Henry, who footed the weekly newspaper bill, was

glowering and trying to read the front page across the length of the table, but it kept slipping at the fold, and his sense of outrage was gradually building up.

'I don't know why I bother to have the thing delivered,' he moaned. 'I never get a chance to look at it. You grab it before it's half-way through the bloody letter-box.'

'Look, if I didn't grab it first, I'd never get a shufty. Any time now you'll be trotting off to the bog with it for half an hour, and I'll be off to work before you surface again.'

Henry's face registered contempt. 'Trust you to talk filth like that when there's food on the table. Anyway, what happens when I do get it, eh? I spend half my time getting bloody marmalade and butter off of it.'

Ben buried his head and munched on, his silence indicating that the morning's verbal battle was over and would not be renewed.

Henry whined. 'You could move it more to the middle and not hog it all. At least I could see the news then.'

Ben pushed the teapot and marmalade a foot forward and managed to leave a sticky smear on the paper. 'Don't know why you bother with all that stuff on the front anyway. The Prime Minister says we're now over the hump and from now on we will have a fleet of Rolls-Royces and yachts, fifty-two weeks holiday a year and pay packets we'll have to carry home on ten ton lorries. You can't believe a bloody word of it.'

'Well, you can this,' said Henry smugly. 'There's a bit here you'll be real pleased to hear about. Make your little day a real holiday.'

'Well either tell me or wrap up, Dad. Don't keep rabbiting on as if it's some kind of quiz game.'

'Well,' said Henry pontifically, 'it says here that your referee pal was knocked off last night.'

'Serves him right. He deserved to get duffed up if you ask

92

me.' And Ben was just about to announce that he had done it, when his father said, 'Oh, no mate, it's a little bit more serious than that. Someone killed him, stone dead.'

Ben experienced momentary shock – not at the magnitude of his offence, but the fact that a brawny bugger like Hudson should have died over what appeared to him no more than a good duffing up. He hastily turned the newspaper round to read it in more detail. He scanned the report avidly and was relieved to find it contained no hint or reference to anything that could possibly associate him or Jeannie with the killing.

Henry said, 'He is the bloke you were all bitching about?'

'Look here, don't you start making snide cracks like that. There's such a thing as the laws of libel and slander so you'd better button up, even if you are my old man. See?'

Henry smacked his forehead with the open palm of a hand. 'Christ. I can't even open my mouth without you jumping down my throat. What did I say that ain't in the paper anyway? You can't deny you said yourself he needed his arse kicking.'

'Kicking someone's arse ain't quite the same as killing him, Dad. I wouldn't go along with that kind of thing, not if he had awarded a hundred and one penalties against us,' he said craftily.

Already his mind was working furiously. The law, he knew only too well, didn't let things like this slide by without pulling out all stops to rope someone in. They weren't to know Hudson wasn't meant to be croaked. Not that that would worry the fuzz a lot. As long as they pinned it on a bloke and got a pat on the back from a judge, that was all *they* cared about.

'Tell you what, Ben,' his father broke in. 'They won't take this little lot lying down. You know what I think...'

'Look, Dad, wrap up for two minutes. A lot of people are going to say they heard me say what I thought of him. Now that isn't exactly going to count in my favour, is it? Even though I know fuck all about it.'

Henry sighed exaggeratedly. 'It's lucky your Mum isn't home to hear you use such language.'

Normally Ben enjoyed the morning altercations with his father, and the needling gave him a great deal of satisfaction, but with so much to think about and plan he wanted to cut it short. So he tossed the newspaper across the table.

'Go on in the throne room and give yourself a goad read in comfort.'

Henry rose. 'You must have got out of bed the wrong side,' was his parting quip.

Ben poured a fresh cup of tea, and sat down to draw up a line of action that would provide him with a water-tight alibi. Although he had never fallen foul of the law himself, he knew enough about them from people who had, to anticipate the way their minds worked. Anyway, there were enough television plays and films around that showed what clever sods they were. They just ganged up with scientists and fingerprint experts and whatnot, and hounded you down. And when they did catch up they just belted seven bells out of you until you coughed. And if you didn't, they hung a verbal on.

But they could be beat. You just needed to stay one jump ahead. And he was quietly confident he was more than a match for any fuzz. That didn't mean *you* could underestimate them though, and one thing hit him like a seven-pound hammer – every bit of evidence that could possibly connect him with it would have to be got rid of – sharpish.

Then there was Jeannie to brief. So long as they both had the same story, and stuck to it like mud on a cow's arse, they were both home and dry. Without any doubt Caleb was the weak link, and they would really have to put the frighteners on him, or he would break like a dried up old twig.

As he was wearing the same clothes he had worn the night before, he returned to his bedroom and began to scrutinise them inch by inch, as if looking for fleas. There were some brownish stains on his trousers that could have come from the garage – on the other hand they could be blood, so he decided to take no chances and completely changed, even to his underclothes, and socks. Then he went out on to the balcony from where he could see his padlocked scooter. He would just have to take a chance that no one had seen him use it the previous night. It was impossible to cater for everything, but Lady Luck was on his side, for he had got back so late that he had cut the engine and wheeled it in to avoid windows being thrown open, and neighbours shouting, 'Have a bit of consideration and stop that bloody noise.'

Reluctantly he decided that the scooter would have to be written off.

Rummaging in the larder, he found a plastic carrier bag into which he rammed his clothing, then he hammered on the toilet door and shouted, 'Dad! There's something I forgot to tell you.'

Henry snapped back, 'You take the ticket sometimes. Can't it wait till I've finished?'

'Keep your shirt on. I've got to go out early, that's all. I didn't mention it before in case it worried you, but someone nicked my scooter yesterday'

'Is that all? Why should it worry me?'

'Just thought I'd let you know, that's all. Well, I'm off to the nick to report.'

Before approaching the scooter, he had a careful look around to see if anyone was observing him, and as far as he could see no one was about.

Cautiously he wheeled the scooter out through a narrow back alley exit. A route he normally never took. But then neither did anyone else. It led across a deserted patch of rubbish-strewn ground that was destined at some future date for housing development. At one stage during the war it had been turned into allotments, when the national appeal to 'Dig for Victory' had been zealously answered. Now the sole reminder of this era was a ramshackle hut of corrugated iron and asbestos that housed a wheel barrow, spades and forks, runner-bean poles, and sacks of fertilisers. Ben manoeuvred the scooter inside and covered it with an evil-smelling sack. Behind the plot wound a disused canal, a snail's pace stretch of pewter-coloured water. It was a safe hiding place, for no one ever visited the area now.

He walked round to Jeannie's home and waited patiently on the corner until she left for work. His muted whistle halted her as she walked briskly towards a bus stop. She turned and hurried back to him, blurting out, 'Did you hear the news? What are we going to do? I was in two minds whether or not to come round to see you.'

'Just as well you didn't. No point in getting all worked up about it. It's just one of those unlucky things. What we've got to do is stick together with one story, and no matter what happens don't budge from it. If we keep our cool no one can touch us.'

Jeannie noticed his grip on her arm was far tighter than normal. 'Can you get the morning off?' he asked.

'I suppose so, but they won't go a bundle on it. We're so short-handed at the moment. But I could ring the forewoman and say my periods are playing me up or something. Why?'

'First things first. Is your old man still at home?'

"Course not. He goes out early.'

'Good, 'cos what you've got to do is belt back and get all the gear you were wearing last night. I've got mine here. Then take it round to a launderette and bung it in with one of those new powders that take out everything. Then put it in the drier. After that take it all to one of those do-it-yourself dry cleaners. That'll get rid of any blood or things. 'Cos it's a dead cert that if they ever get around to feeling our collars, that's the kind of thing they'll look for. Our boots is the first thing they'll look at, so there mustn't be a trace of anything on them.'

Jeannie said, 'That'll mean changing. But if you say so. The cleaners is a fab idea though. I often have to go round there with my dad's stuff. So no one will think it fishy.'

'Why should anyone think that anyway? That's what the bloody place is for. Then I'm off to the nick to report my scooter was pinched yesterday. But I'll brief you on that later. Next we got to get alongside Caleb and put the fear of Christ into him.'

Jeannie made her telephone call and a sympathetic fore-woman told her to, 'Stay home till you feel better.'

Ben went to clock on, and having done so told the charge-hand he was off to the police station to report the loss of his scooter.

The charge-hand retorted, 'Why bother to clock on? You could have called on the police on your way in, surely?'

'I didn't know how long it takes, do I now? No point in losing money over it, is there?'

The brown-walled police station was one of hundreds that were built around the same period, when the national economy was in a parlous state and public spending was pruned to a minimum. Inside, it was all olive green and white paint. On the left of the entrance passage was a door marked 'Enquiries'.

A thick oak counter ran the whole width of the room which was cluttered with desks and battered typewriters. There were posters everywhere offering or seeking information.

'Right, son,' called the sergeant.

Ben lolled against the counter. 'I want to report the theft of a motor scooter.'

With a sigh, the officer humped a big ledger on to the counter. Ben dictated his name and address, the make and registration number of the machine, along with a description of its colour and outstanding marks of identification.

'Approximate time, and place it was stolen from.'

'I can't say the exact time. But some time early last night. At a rough guess I'd say it was about sixish because I used it to get home from work. Then I went out with my girl. It wasn't there when I got back.'

'Wasn't where?'

'The place I always keep it in the flats where I live.'

'You've left it long enough before coming here. Obviously didn't worry you over much, eh?'

'It wasn't that. I spent most of last night scouring the streets. You see, I thought one of my mates had been skylarking about and took it for a joke. Anyway, I didn't come sooner as I know how busy you are.'

The sergeant was non-committal at this unexpected show of consideration.

'Driving licence, and insurance,' he demanded.

Ben handed them over the counter for the sergeant to examine and copy down the details.

'You're dead right when you say I wasn't too worried. You can see I'm insured, and so I'll get my money back.'

As he handed the licence and cover note back, the sergeant said, 'It's not as easy as that, son. It'll be some time before the insurance company accepts that it has been stolen. It'll probably turn up a bit battered, but not a write-off. The insurance company will pay for any repairs without carping, but they won't rush to fork out for a new one. Naturally you will have to inform them without delay.'

Ben left perturbed by the unexpected turn of events. He had not anticipated any trouble from the insurance company. His original plan had been to dump the scooter in the canal. But now he was in two minds about it. Maybe it would be better to leave it in the hut. Then if nothing ever happened, he could pick it up later and carry on as usual. It was a problem, and no mistake, and would have to be given a lot of thought. It was no good acting rash and cocking things up. Meanwhile, there was Jeannie to meet and Caleb to sort out.

He whiled away the time in a cafe where he drank a cup of tea and smoked three cigarettes, and read all the papers that had been left lying around on the oil-cloth covered tables. They all carried reports of the murder.

When Jeannie rejoined him, she said, 'I don't think anyone could find a thing on them now. Not that I think it was necessary in my case. I had a good look at my gear when I read about it, and I couldn't see a thing on anything.'

'You couldn't, but the law can find things you can't see with the naked eye. They got special microscopes and Christ knows how many tests to find clues.'

'Well, we just can't sit here nattering. What are we going to do with this clobber?'

'Take it home, of course. No one is in at my place, and your old man is at work so there's no problem there. Then we had better go back to work. After that we'll sort out Caleb. No point in arousing suspicion by going to see him at work.'

'Feel like coming round to our place for a little while first?'

'What for?' asked Ben.

'What do you think? It's time we did it. We might not get such a good chance again. Or you chicken you might put me in the family way?' she giggled.

'Come off it, Jeannie. You won't be the first girl I've screwed.' He lied, but it sounded so convincing that Jeannie retorted, 'It better not be someone I know. I tell you that straight.'

'You don't know her, so forget it. See you in twenty minutes.'

They lay naked in the big double bed still cherished by Jeannie's father. They had made love first clumsily, then to their mutual satisfaction. Now they were lazily finding the secrets of each other's body with exploring hands.

'Dad would do his nut is he could see us now,' she laughed.

'We should have got round to doing this before,' mused Ben. 'It's not half bad.'

Jeannie cradled closer and found pleasure running her hand over the stubble of his head. 'I wouldn't have minded, but you always acted as if just the thought of it would make you throw up.'

'It didn't seem my scene somehow. A bit kind of sloppy.' His hands caressed her breasts until the nipples responded. 'You've got quite a nice pair, Jeannie. I'd've never guessed it from some of those shirts you wear.'

'Didn't you know? The birds in the gang do all they can to flatten them. We got special bras.'

'If they're like this underneath I couldn't give a monkey's what you wrap them up in during the day.' He chuckled loudly as if over some secret joke. 'Imagine all those poor sods sweating their knackers off at work while we're doing this. Bit of a giggle, really.'

Her hand had coaxed him into tumescence once more. 'I must say, Ben, you're well made.'

There was a hint of anger in his voice. 'How would you know? You must have done this before.'

'Come off it, Ben. This is no time or place to lose your rag. As a matter of fact, I haven't, but it's all the girls at the works ever talk about.'

'Go on!'

'No, honest. They got crumpet on the brain. Drop their pants at a wink. Even in the lunch hour they'll have one. There can't be any men in our place who haven't had it away.'

'We could do with some of them hot pants at my dump. The po-faced bitches in our office never look as if they feel fruity, ever.'

'It's not just sex with them, Ben. They do it for a lark in most cases. One woman even keeps a score card for individual performances. You'd be surprised at some of the ratings.'

'Don't their old men mind?'

'They don't know, silly. They're all on the pill so they don't have to worry.' There was a prolonged silence which prompted Ben to ask, 'What's up with you?'

'I was thinking. If we're going to do this regular don't you think I should go on it? These things you're using aren't fool proof, and I'm in no mad rush to get knocked up.'

So it was agreed that she would call at the Family Planning Clinic at the first convenient opportunity.

They made love again.

'You know, we won't have many chances like this again, though.'

'We can get together when your Dad goes out one night.'

'We are both going to go short of it if we wait for that.

Dad never goes out, or very seldom. Boy, would he do his nut if he saw us at it! He's very old fashioned in some ways. Always on about the evils of it, I wonder if he ever enjoyed it.'

'You talk like you don't like him a lot, Jeannie.'

'I don't.'

Suddenly, and without warning, Ben swung out of bed. 'I'd better be getting back. The gaffer will think I was having him on about the scooter if I'm away any longer.'

When they had dressed, Ben said, 'I'll see you at the disco round seven. Then we'll get alongside Caleb and lean on him – real hard.'

'You going to tell him about our clothes and the scooter?'

'Not sure yet. I'll have to think about it. Maybe it's not good for you and me if everyone is all cleaned up.'

She kissed him at the door. 'See you tonight.'

Chapter XVII

Hudson's death had come as a staggering shock to Caleb, although he had anticipated it a hundred times or more during the seemingly endless night. At first he had lain awake praying that the man had not been badly hurt, but as the hours dragged away in patches of sleep that seemed only minutes long, his fears worsened. And like all night fears, they multiplied with the imperceptible passing of time, until he began to perspire at the thought that they may have killed him. Finally, the fears gave way to a firm conviction that they had. Twice he had been forced to get up and tip-toe into the kitchen to swallow large draughts of water to ease his parched mouth. The second time his father had called, 'Wykeham! You all right? You been in and out there so no one else can sleep, hardly.'

He desperately wanted to relieve his thirst again but dreaded waking his father. As there was no clock in the room he could only guess at the time, and this he shied from doing in case he guessed it was later than it really was. And it was out of the question to steal from his bed into the sitting room, to look at the clock on the mantelpiece. Quite apart from the noise, it would have meant switching on the light, and that would certainly have awakened his father.

So he lay there, clammy with fear, until the first glimmer of light began to filter through the chink in the curtains. Even then it did not help, for he had no idea what time it became light. He only knew it was daylight when his mother called him with a cup of tea to shake him awake. That was regularly at 7.45 a.m., except of course on Saturdays and Sundays, when he was allowed to lie in. In the silence, he could hear his own heart beating, and as he listened to it he became convinced that something was wrong with him, and he put this down to the horrifying effects of the previous night. He secretly hoped that a sudden but painless convulsion would seize him and he could die, and so escape the consequences of what he had done.

He slid quietly out of bed and crossed silently to the window and parted the curtains. The street lights were still burning, although he could see the whole length of the street, which was deserted except for a milkman's battery-powered van, and its driver scurrying from doorstep to doorstep depositing bottles and eggs in containers of compressed cardboard. But *his* presence was no guide to the time, as Caleb was unaware of when he did his rounds.

His ears listened for the questioning voice of his father, but it did not come. Then his eyes focused on the small transistor radio by his bedside. He twiddled the frequency knob in an attempt to pick up a news bulletin, but all he could get was the crackle and whine of static, and in the semi-dark lost the position of the station selector. Finally, he picked up a speaking voice. From the tone of the announcer he knew it was a news bulletin. For one moment, he feared the noise would awaken the family. Finally the announcer said, as if it were a space filler :

'Murder. C.I.D. officers under Detective Chief Superintendent Cyril Porter are investigating the death of Mr Barry Hudson, found battered to death on an open space near his home last night. Mr Hudson, 36, married with three young children, was a football referee. A police spokesman said early this morning, "We are treating this as a case of murder." '

Caleb was still stunned at what he had been so convinced would be announced. He realised he had been *thinking* about death, but really conditioning himself to hear that Hudson – a figure on a football field and a name in a telephone directory – would be said to be in hospital recovering from severe bruises and shock, inflicted by assailants there was no possible chance of tracing.

He switched off the set, suddenly overcome by an irresistible urge to get out of the house before any of the family got up. Caleb was convinced his face would give him away.

His clothes were draped on a chair by his bed, and he hastily dressed, feeling his guilt with every garment he put on. He went into the kitchen and washed and shaved. Then as he had feared, his father's voice came through the door. 'Wykeham, why you up and about so early? Something wrong?'

The quaver in his voice was audible as he called back, 'It's all right, Dad. I was asked to go in early. I didn't

104

mention it last night as I got back so late.'

'You got time to eat, son. No one should go out on an empty stomach.'

'Sorry, haven't got time.'

'I'll put the kettle on while you wash, son.'

He shouted back. 'No. I'm already off.'

'Won't take a minute. Even the Post Office can wait that time.'

But he was already out of the kitchen and heading for the door, dreading the thought of confronting his father and the probing questions he was bound to ask. Caleb was only half-way across the room when his father appeared in his pyjamas.

'Why all the secrecy, son? You only got to ask your mother or me, and we call you. No need for this slipping off without a word to nobody.'

Caleb did not pause in his flight – for it was flight – and he averted his face as he went towards the door, convinced that guilt was etched deeply in his face. 'I'll explain everything, later. No need for a panic just because I get called in early.'

A note of anger was evident in his father's voice as Caleb slipped through the door. 'Wykeham. You come back here. I want...'

As he entered the area, he paused for a few seconds to examine his scooter. One lamp was smashed, and most of the fox's tail was missing. These he would replace at the first opportunity.

On the pavement outside, he drew deep lungfuls of air and stood uncertain which way to walk as he had no set destination, his sole concern being to get out of the house. Because it was the shortest distance to a turning he walked left, fast, almost at a trot, fleeing from the window which he knew would be thrown open, and a voice demanding his return.

Once he had turned the corner he stopped and patted his pockets for cigarettes and found a packet with three inside. But he had no matches. His feet echoed on the pavement as he scurried along, eyes searching for someone who could provide the indispensable light. It came from a man on a cycle he flagged down. The man dismounted and laboriously adjusted the pedal against the kerb until the cycle was safely parked.

'What's up, son?'

'Have you got a light, please?'

Exasperation registered on the man's face. 'Christ, you didn't stop me for that! I've been up all night.'

'Sorry,' he mumbled.

'It's too late to be sorry now. You ought to be able to do without at your age,' he grumbled, patting his jacket and then his trouser pockets. 'You're out of luck. I should have a box, but I can't find them.'

Caleb waited patiently while he renewed his patting before producing a box from his breast pocket. 'Funny. Don't usually keep them there.'

Caleb concealed his mounting annoyance as the man fumbled through the box, producing one spent match after another which he tossed away. 'Bad habit of mine that. Putting the dead ones back, I mean.' When he did produce a live match, Caleb tried to control the trembling of his hands as he cupped them round the flame the man proffered.

'You are in a right state, and no mistake, son. It's not a fag you want – it's a nerve tonic.'

Caleb offered one of the remaining two cigarettes to the man, who declined with a wave of his hand. 'Too early for me. All I want is a cup of tea and some shut-eye.'

The man pedalled off, wobbling at first, then steadying

as he gained momentum. Caleb walked on, inhaling deeply. As the cigarette neared its end he lighted another from its tip, wishing he had some matches which would enable him to conserve his meagre stock. Then he realised it did not matter – sooner or later he would come across a newsagent's shop. There he could get both cigarettes and matches – *and* a newspaper. It was some minutes before he came across a shop where a shirt-sleeved man with sleep-lidded eyes was writing numbers and street names on the top of newspapers. As the shopkeeper took down the cigarettes from the shelf behind him, Caleb said, 'I'll have a paper too.'

Once clear of the shop, Caleb stopped and repeatedly read the story, as if with each fresh scrutiny some new facts would emerge, or the magnitude of his crime would in some miraculous manner be diminished. No new facts emerged, however, and his sense of guilt merely increased until it assumed almost unbearable proportions. So much so that his brain became numbed, and he entered an almost trance-like state, unaware in which direction he was heading, and devoid of any destination. He walked on aimlessly and mechanically, until he emerged into reality once more, and became aware of familiar surroundings. Confronting him was the spire of St Michael and All Angels, the church where they regularly worshipped.

Suddenly the impulse to go inside was overwhelming. Church was *the* place to go when you were in trouble. As he entered the dimly lit, almost gloomy building, that smelt faintly of incense, he automatically dipped his fingers into the stone bowl containing holy water, and crossed himself.

In a far corner he saw the flicker of candles caught in an unseen draught, and decided to offer one to Hudson's memory. Rashly he dropped a ten penny piece into the coin box, and placed a candle on the stand. He knelt on the padded knee rest, crossed himself and whispered, 'May the

107

souls of the faithful departed, rest in peace. Amen.' Caleb had little interest in Hudson's departed spirit for he could recall nothing of the man except his terrified face illuminated by the spot-lamps of the scooters. His death was merely the cause of the all-consuming fear for his own safety which now gripped him. And because he realised this only too well, he had paid so lavishly for the candle. The gesture would appear commendable in God's eyes.

A hand touched his shoulder, and he heard a voice say softly, 'It must have been someone you loved dearly. Wykeham, isn't it?'

Caleb remained kneeling and turned his head to see one of the priests standing behind him. The pale face, topped by a balding head, was familiar to him, but he could not attach a name to it.

Caleb made as if to rise, but the hand on his shoulder increased its pressure, restraining him. 'Don't let me interrupt your meditations.'

'I've finished now,' mumbled Caleb, and the pressure relaxed. The priest only remembered his name because the youth was one of the few coloured members of the congregation, and he felt compelled to go out of his way to remember as many as he could. He knew, rather guiltily, that it was an inverted form of prejudice.

'I did not see you at Mass,' said the priest. 'Were you here?'

'No, Father. I just happened to be passing so I dropped in.'

The priest racked his mind to recall someone who had died recently, who meant so much to the boy, for he was visibly agitated, but no name would come readily to mind. Still, he couldn't be expected to remember every death, and he consoled himself with the thought that it had probably been someone in a different parish, or even the home land

108

of the boy's parents. They were, he mused, an emotional people.

Caleb rose. 'I have a problem, Father.'

The priest thought of his waiting breakfast, and hoped that the lad wouldn't decide to burden him with it here and now. It was probably some trivial misdeed that lay heavy on his conscience for the time being. A feather-weight burden that could be lifted by a few Hail Mary's or a decade of the rosary.

'There is no burden that isn't halved with sharing, Wykeham,' said the priest.

Caleb knew the importance and value of the confession. But was murder different? Would he be expected to go voluntarily to the police and confess? Would the priest point out that he was absolved from guilt in the eyes of God, but not the law? And the law was what troubled him most.

He decided to sound out the priest. 'Actually, Father, when I say a problem it's not actually mine. It's a close friend who is in very deep trouble.'

'I appreciate your concern for this friend, whoever he may be, but I can hardly help him through an intermediary.'

The words meant nothing to Caleb, but the meaning was clear – if he wanted help he would have to be completely honest, which at this stage he was not prepared to be.

'I'll have a word with him, Father. And thanks.'

'Tell your friend not to waste too much time.' And, as if an afterthought, he added, 'While you are here, Wykeham, is there anything *you* would like to talk over with me?'

Caleb told him there was not and hurried out, still feeling the grip of the handshake.

A sense of disappointment invaded him when he reached the street once again. There had been no miraculous solution to the problem which tormented him. His thoughts turned to Ben and he felt encouraged. *He* would have all the answers. You could bet that Ben wasn't walking around in a cold funk. He would be at work as usual, just as if nothing had happened.

Caleb headed for the garage where Ben worked. It was a long walk, but he did not mind for there was no point in getting there too early. On the way he tried to recall anything that might connect him with the crime. But there was nothing. The only visible reminders of the previous night were a damaged headlamp and one half of an imitiation tail. But thousands of youngsters rode scooters and many must have broken lamps, while the tail was no more than a symbol that could be seen fluttering from countless machines.

When he reached the garage he realised he had taken the walk too easily, for men were already busy at work and it had been his intention to stop Ben on the way in. He recognised Ben's charge-hand and walked over to ask casually, 'Ben in yet?'

'No.'

'He ain't sick, is he?'

'No such bloody luck. He's clocked on. But he had to go and see the police.'

The man walked away before Caleb could question him further. The announcement terrified Caleb, for it could only mean one thing. The fuzz had gotten on to something and had asked Ben to go and see them.

For one moment he thought of going to the station and waiting outside; until he realised the folly of this. Now was no time to panic. He must act and carry on as if nothing had happened. Quickening his step, he hurried to the Post Office where he worked. Already he had decided to be patient until the evening when he would go to the disco and

110

wait for Ben to turn up. He was confident Ben had had an answer to all the cops' questions.

The day went as any other at the Post Office. Hudson's name was not even mentioned.

When the opportunity presented itself, he went to the rack of telephone directories and ripped out the page on which he had circled Hudson's name. As he turned he almost knocked over the foreman.

'Sorry,' said Caleb. 'I didn't hear you come up behind.'

'You seem to spend a lot of time looking at that book. You got yourself a girl in that area?'

'Something like that,' said Caleb, and as he walked away he saw the foreman looking at the directory. But the command he was expecting to come back and explain the missing page, never came, and he assumed the foreman had not noticed it. That at least, he thought, showed that luck had not entirely deserted him.

Chapter XVIII

When the three of them finally met at the discotheque, it was too crowded to talk freely, for no sooner had Ben taken his customary seat at the corner table than he was surrounded by members of the gang all anxious to talk about the murder. They were so nervously boisterous and jocular, that Ben feared they would attract attention.

'It's one for the book all right, Ben,' said one youth. 'Who'd have thought he'd cop his lot like that. Serves him right.'

Another said knowingly, 'I hope the law don't come sniffing round here thinking we had something to do with

111

it.' Although he was innocent he made it sound as if a visit from the police would be disastrous. Ben realised that he just wanted to give the impression that he knew more about it than he could reveal. It was sheer bravado, but it could be dangerous.

'Why don't you shut your bloody cake hole for a minute,' snapped Ben.

'It's silly buggers like you blabbering that put thoughts in people's heads,' said an outraged Jeannie.

'Don't get shirty with us,' said another youth. 'Can't we even talk? So what if the law do come round? It's not down to us, is it? I mean, we had nothing to do with it.' A note of doubt crept into his voice when he saw Ben's expression.

It prompted a boy who had been arrested after the scene outside the football ground to protest, 'I got fined £25 for kicking his car. Some nosey copper might think of putting two and two together and connecting me with it.'

Caleb's anxiety was mounting all the time. Ben was playing it real cool, he thought, and he was dying to ask him about the visit to the police station; but obviously this was not the time and place. Well, he would prove to them that he could keep *his* cool and not panic as they were always so fond of saying.

Ben stood up, 'I had nothing to do with it, and can prove it. So the first one I hear saying anything out of line will get his teeth kicked in. O.K.?'

The silence that followed was confirmation that no one would take the risk of even hinting that there might be some association.

'We're going off to talk private. Just the three of us. And if you characters have got any nous you won't natter about this at all. Not even among yourselves. Just act like it didn't exist. That silly git there was talking like he *wanted* to have his collar felt.' With that he tugged Jeannie to her

112

feet and shouldered his way out.

Outside Caleb asked, 'Where we going to talk, Ben?'

'I dunno. Some quiet boozer. We got a lot to go over.'

'Righteo. You lead, I'll follow,' said Caleb, straddling his scooter.

'I ain't got mine with me,' said Ben, as if there was no significance in the fact at all. 'Anyway, you won't need it. We're not going far.'

Caleb said, 'Ben, about the police . . .'

Ben cut him short. 'Now don't you bloody start.'

They tried several public houses before they found one with a deserted public bar. There Ben told Caleb to order three rum and Cokes, while he and Jeannie sat down in a corner out of ear's distance of the bar.

'What plans we got, Ben?' asked Caleb as he put the drinks down.

'None. What plans can we have? It's just a question of playing wait-and-see and watching which way the cookie crumbles. The way I see it is this – we've got nothing to worry about just so long as we don't panic. And that's where you come in.'

'Me!'

'Yes, you, mate. The only trouble is going to come if someone's bottle goes, and quite frankly it'll be you if it's anybody.'

Jeannie backed him up. 'Let's face it, Caleb, you'll be the first to run to panic stations.'

'Look, I'm in this just as much as you two. So don't think I'm going to do anything that'll upset things.'

'Good for you, Caleb, because that's just what we wanted to talk to you about. You see, Jeannie and me are in the clear. We can back up each other's story that we wasn't there. So it's two against one really. Got the message?'

Caleb rose in anger. 'Now don't you try putting the

finger on me, the pair of you.'

'Sit down, you big prick. No sooner does anyone say anything to you than you start carrying on in the way we're all scared you will.'

Caleb resumed his seat, sulkily silent. It was a silence he could not maintain. 'Look, Ben, why are you keeping things from me? I know the fuzz have seen you already. You went to the nick this morning.'

Ben sighed in an exaggerated manner. 'It wasn't about this, you daft bleeder. Someone nicked my scooter if you must know. It was as simple as that.' For some inexplicable reason, Ben decided not to tell him the motive behind it, for somewhere at the back of his mind was the thought that it would be useful to him later on. He didn't want Caleb to go rushing round reporting his was missing too. The law would really smell something fishy then. And again the thought crossed his mind that it would not be too smart of him to let Caleb put himself in the clear.

It was as if Jeannie had read his thoughts, for she leaned forward and whispered, 'Look. All you've got to remember is that it's two against one if you go chicken. Remember, you were the one who did the real damage. Didn't he, Ben?'

'In all honesty, I'd have to go along with Jeannie on that.'

'But,' protested Caleb, 'you two did more than me. I only gave one kick. God's honour.'

'That's what *you* say, Caleb. Not what we know. If it came to the pinch we would have to protect ourselves. Two against one, just like we said. And you're coloured too, which don't help. I know who the law will believe. You know how they got a down on the coloureds.'

Caleb said wearily, 'O.K. Ben. 'You just tell me what you want me to do. I'll do it.'

114

'Nothing. Precisely nothing. We just sit tight and wait. In my opinion, nothing will happen. It'll all blow over. But we must keep real mum about things. If you wipe your arse with your right hand, your left one mustn't even know. It's as bad as that.'

They had two more drinks before Ben called the meeting to a close. 'There's just one other thing,' he said. 'I don't think we should be seen around too much with each other. No point in drawing attention. If anything important crops up we can always arrange a meet or get a message passed.'

Caleb felt let down and betrayed. From the way the conversation had gone he was fully aware that Ben and Jeannie would not hesitate to pin the blame on him, but he could not see any way around this. As they said, it was their word against his.

A few streets away from the pub, they saw a handwritten poster at an evening newspaper stand which stated: *Vital new clues in Ref murder.*

Ben was unperturbed. From past experience he knew the posters were deliberately misleading, so that when you read, 'Famous Hollywood star found dead', you knew it would turn out to be an old lady of eighty who danced in the Ziegfeld Follies. But Caleb was unable to resist running across the street and buying a newspaper. The story stated that the police had revealed that two vital clues had been found at the murder scene. They were part of an imitation fox tail, such as used for decorative purposes on motor scooters and the glass from a headlamp.

Caleb handed the paper to Ben. 'Look at that. What am I going to say if they find my machine with a busted lamp, and the tail thing too? You tell me that, Ben.'

'If you've got any sense, Caleb, you'll see to it that the lamp and the other thing are replaced.'

Jeannie slapped him on the back with a gesture that contained more warning than encouragement. 'Just like we said, Caleb. Things don't look too good for you.'

As she and Ben went off arm-linked and whispering, Caleb misconstrued this new intimacy as a sign that they were ganging up on him. He thought to himself. 'They're cooking up something.'

As soon as he had retrieved his machine, he rode home and decided not to touch it until he had replaced the lamp glass and tail.

And when his father tried to question him about the morning, he pleaded a sick headache and went straight into his room, and bed. There he lay with the radio ear-plug inserted, listening anxiously for any new announcement. He fell asleep with it in his ear. It was still connected when his mother woke him with a cup of tea.

Chapter XIX

Porter was now convinced that Hudson's death was linked with soccer hooligans, which had accounted for his deliberately releasing to the Press the information about the two clues. What at first had seemed an extremely difficult case now looked comparatively simple. It was, he ruminated, just a question of pressing ahead with the routine enquiries until something hard was unearthed, and maintaining a non-stop war of nerves against the culprits. It was what he called, 'putting on the frighteners'.

His painstaking routine work had already produced two firm leads: a list of names of the youths who had appeared in court following the incident after the game, and statements from the man who had been attacked on the train and his eye-witness friend. Both had mentioned a big coloured lad. And over the telephone he had talked with the inspector who had actually witnessed the attack on Hudson's car. He, too, made an ominous reference to 'a big coloured lay-about'.

Porter had laid on two police vans to round up as many of the youths as possible and take them to the police station near the Rovers ground, where he and his sergeant would interview them; while the young C.I.D. aide Wilcox had been sent to the area where they lived with instructions to sniff around for information.

'These kids are all Rovers supporters. See if they have some common meeting place. A pub or something. Chat the guvnor up at opening time.'

Wilcox had not been in the neighbourhood of the Rovers ground half an hour before his casual street corner enquiries led him to 'The Penalty Spot'.

A blousy barmaid in mule slipper and hair curlers was reading a newspaper on the bar.

Wilcox rapped the counter with the edge of a coin. 'Pint of mild and bitter, please.'

She looked up and said, 'Crikey. Can't you sleep?' and as if to emphasise her astonishment glanced at the bar clock running the accepted ten minutes fast. 'Or is it the hair of the dog?'

Wilcox said, 'Is the guvnor around?'

The clock seemed to be the barometer of all her emotions, for she looked at it again and said, 'You must be jo-king, love. He don't get down till about twelve. This place is a bone orchard till then.'

'Bone orchard?'

'Cemetery.' Again she consulted the clock. 'Twelve on the dot. I mean, look at *me*. You don't think I'd traipse

117

around looking like this if there was customers to serve, do you?'

Wilcox said, 'You look charming. Have a drink?'

'Flattery will get you everywhere,' she said. 'It's a bit early, but I'll have a glass of sweet stout.' As she unstoppered it on an opener attached to the bar, she said, 'You'll be dead lucky if he comes down. He's pretty set in his habits. You a rep by any chance?'

'No. Do I look it?'

'Yes,' she said bluntly. 'The only well dressed men we get around here at this time of day are either reps or villains. You don't look like a villain to me.'

'I'm afraid I can't discuss the nature of my visit,' he said rather pompously.

'I beg *your* pardon,' she said huffily. 'I'll give him a shout, but there's no guarantee he'll come down.'

Wilcox waited while she went to a food lift, put her head inside and shouted up the shaft, 'Mr Jack, someone to see you.'

A muffled voice came down. 'Ask him what he wants.'

'He won't say.'

There was more than an edge of anger in the voice which came down the shaft, 'He's not a bloody rep is he?'

'He *says* he isn't.'

The verbal exchange ended, and the barmaid turned and said, 'You'll just have to wait and see if he'll come down. He's not one to be rushed. I've done all I can, love.'

'Not to worry,' said Wilcox. 'I'm used to waiting.'

But he was not kept waiting long. The landlord came down in his shirt sleeves and glowered at the neatly attired Wilcox. 'If you're a bloody rep I'll be on to your firm complaining. I *never* see any reps this time of day.'

Wilcox said, 'I'm not hawking anything,' and opened his wallet and flashed his warrant card. 'C.I.D.'

'That's different. Why didn't you say so in the first place? I'd have asked you upstairs.'

'That's all right, Mr Jack. I can talk to you here.'

Mr Jack propped his elbows on the bar, then turned his head and said to the barmaid, 'You might just as well go up and change now I'm down here.'

When she had gone, he said, 'Well, what brings you down to this part of the world? We've been behaving, haven't we?'

'As far as I know you have. I'm making enquiries into the murder of Mr Barry Hudson. I have reason to believe you can help.'

Mr Jack nearly choked on his drink. 'Me – Christ, all I know is what I've read.'

Wilcox realised he was going about it in a ham-fisted way. The last thing he wanted to do was antagonise or frighten the landlord. His tone mellowed: 'Between you and me, and I don't want this to go any further...' The vigorous nodding of Mr Jack's head was intended to convey the impression that red hot irons and thumb screws would not make him divulge the conversation to anyone ... 'Our enquiries lead us to believe that a bunch of local youths who support the club over the road come in here.'

The relief showed in Mr Jack's face. 'Some of the yobos do use the public bar, but they're all mouth. Talk big but do bugger all. I've never had any trouble from them.'

Wilcox said, 'Some lads were picked up after the cup match for tear-arsing around. Any of them come in?'

Mr Jack brushed his stubbled chin. 'I did hear about it, but frankly I don't know their names. They just come in, have a drink, play the juke box, then shove off. And believe you me, I don't try to keep them. Glad to see the back of them.'

'They got a ringleader?'

119

'Well, I suppose you could say that Little Ben Clegg is. Little Ben – that's a joke. He'd make two of me. He's built like a brick shit house. Lives in the new estate. Don't know the number off hand.'

Wilcox jotted down the name, and was disappointed that the landlord did not know his full address, but he could soon get it by looking it up in the local electoral register. The name had not been among those youths who had appeared in court, but if he was the ringleader, it was well worth passing it on to Superintendent Porter.

They chatted on for a few minutes, and then Wilcox suddenly realised he had not asked the question upon which Porter had laid so much stress.

'Oh, one other thing. Do you get a big coloured kid in at all?'

'You don't mean Caleb?'

'I wouldn't know his name, but if he's coloured I'm interested.'

'Well, he's the only one we get. Big gormless bugger who follows Ben around like a bloody dog. I wouldn't put anything past that one,' he said, and added gratuitously: 'Real violent. The kind you don't turn your back on down a dark alley.'

Mr Jack had no reason for suggesting that Caleb was of a violent disposition, he merely felt obliged to say something of value to prove he was anxious and ready to help. And he was blithely unaware that the remark had sent a tremor of excitement through the young officer. It was doubtful if he would have recanted if he had known.

'Caleb, you say?' said Wilcox, as he wrote it down in his note-book. 'What's his surname?'

'There I can't help. As a matter of fact, Caleb is his nickname. I've never heard him called anything else. Me, I've always thought it was offensive, like nigger or spade,

120

but he seems to lap it up,' said Mr Jack.

'What about the address then?'

'There again I'm stuck.' Mr Jack shrugged. 'You know what it's like. People come in, you get to know their first name and that's about all. When they go through that door they cease to exist as far as I'm concerned. Good riddance to bad rubbish in his case.'

'No clues at all?'

'Yes there is, come to think of it.' He scraped his stubbled chin. 'Works at the Post Office. I saw him wearing one of their badges on his coat. Don't say I told you. Can't say I approve of these coloureds cornering all the good jobs when our own kind are unemployed. You've only got to look at the buses, tubes and railways to realise they'll be making a take-over bid soon. But you say anything, and you're not a patriot but a nigger baiter. That's why I'd be grateful if you didn't let it be known where that little bit of information came from.'

Wilcox assured him that he wouldn't, and then in turn demanded an assurance from Mr Jack that he would not discuss the visit with any of his customers.

The young aide was so convinced that he was on the brink of a major development in the case that he hailed a taxi, and told the driver to take him to the police station where Porter was interviewing the rounded up youths.

Porter was sitting in a borrowed office drinking tea with Sergeant Rowan after a frustrating couple of hours interviewing the youths. They had all been surly, cocky, uncooperative and not at all worried or overawed at being interrogated. Questioned about their court appearance they had all adhered to the same monotonous and untruthful story – they had nothing to do with the rumpus outside the ground; they just happened to be passing when the police had

121

nabbed them for no reason at all. Just spite.

They had been seen individually, and were now waiting in a large room until the vans turned up to return them to where they were picked up. They sat smoking, giggling and treating it all as a huge joke.

Wilcox could hardly keep the excitement from his voice. 'I think I've found your coloured bloke, sir.'

Porter waved him to a seat. 'Take it easy, son. Now tell me what makes you think he's the one we're looking for.'

Wilcox recounted the conversation in the public house, with special emphasis on the fact that Mr Jack had mentioned Caleb had a violent disposition. As a make weight, he also mentioned Ben, but did not attach a great deal of importance to that.

Porter remained silent for a while, then turned to his sergeant. 'Well, what do you think of it, George? Violent, coloured, goes to football. Moves around in a pack. Certainly fits in with what we know.'

Rowan said, 'It's certainly worth turning him over, sir. Let's face it, we've had no joy at all with this little lot we pulled in. All case-hardened bloody liars. Let's have Caleb in, and I'd like to have a few words with this Ben, too.'

Porter rose. 'Let's go to the Post Office.'

At the Post Office, Porter asked to see the supervisor, and when he was ushered into his office he enquired if they had a coloured lad called Caleb, working there.

The supervisor said, 'I think there is one in the sorting department, but the best man to see is the foreman. He's more in direct touch than I am.'

When the foreman came in, Porter said, 'I'd rather like to talk to this young Caleb chap. Could you ask him to step in here.'

The foreman said, 'You don't mean young Wykeham, do you? He's the only coloured boy we've got.'

122

'If he rides a scooter, likes football and wears big boots, he's the one.'

'That sounds like him,' said the foreman. 'But he isn't in at the moment. I told him to take a couple of days off. Something's upset the lad I think. Very fidgety, can't concentrate. Bit of girl trouble if you ask me. I sent him home because he was no use to me mooning around here in a trance.'

Porter exchanged a knowing glance with Rowan. 'Something's bothering him? Well, that tallies. If it's not too much trouble, I'd like his home address, straight away.'

The foreman assured him it was no trouble at all, and returned with it in a few minutes. 'Is it all right to ask why you want all this?'

'Not at the moment,' said Porter. 'You mentioned girl trouble. What makes you say that?'

The foreman twisted an ear and looked sheepish. 'Nothing really. When a lad starts going around in a trance, that's what you automatically think.' He paused. 'Well, that isn't strictly true. But I noticed he came in here on his day off, and went to the rack of telephone directories. He was mucking about round them again later. I suppose I was being nosey, but I asked him if he had a girl friend. I assumed he had, because when I looked at the book he had torn the page out. I was going to speak to him about it, say he could have copied the number down without ruining the book, but it slipped my mind.'

Rowan said, 'I think we ought to have a look at the book, don't you, sir?'

Porter nodded, and the foreman took them to the rack and pointed out the directory. 'That's the one. Look, I hope I'm not dropping the boy in anything. I only remember it was this one because I made a note to replace it. I know it struck me at the time that he had certainly picked a girl who lived far enough away, but then youngsters don't have to worry about distance as we did when we courted. They can get anywhere on those scooter things of theirs.'

Porter and Rowan both knew exactly what they were looking for as they turned the pages of the book; both experienced a feeling of achievement when they found the page containing the Hudsons was missing.

Porter said, 'I'm afraid we'll have to take this with us. My sergeant will also have to take a statement from you later to the effect that you saw this young lad looking at this directory, and the fact that a page was missing directly afterwards.'

A bewildered foreman asked, 'Am I allowed to know what I'm letting him in for?'

'Not at this stage I'm afraid,' said Porter. 'And I must insist that you don't discuss this at all with anyone.'

On the journey to Caleb's home, there was a detectable note of optimism in their conversation, as if they were aware that they were nearing the end of the enquiry, and the net was fast closing around their quarry.

Chapter XX

Caleb was lying on his bed chain smoking and staring at the smoke as it curled towards the ceiling, his mind a complete blank. An untouched cup of coffee stood on a bedside table gathering a scum of milk. He was rapidly approaching breaking point. Since being sent home, he had done nothing but mope around the flat, or loll spiritlessly on his bed in an almost comatose state.

His mother padded quietly into the bedroom and removed the cold coffee. 'Can I made you some soup, son?' she asked solicitously.

He rolled over to hide his face from her gaze. 'No. How many times have I got to tell you to leave me alone?'

'I think I should call the doctor. It's not natural for a boy to laze around not eating or talking. You must be sickening for a fever.' When she placed her hand on his brow, he brushed it away with such venom that she flinched, and recoiled in fear.

'Get your hands off of me,' he screamed.

'I was only feeling for a fever, son,' she said, and began to weep quietly. 'What we going to do with you? You don't want nothing and won't say nothing for us to help even. If you in trouble we all got a right to know. It's no good that the whole house be upset for one person.'

She sat on the foot of his bed waiting for him to speak, but there was no response from Caleb who just wanted to be left alone, believing that if he could only shut out everything, his problems would disappear, just as a chair did when he closed his eyes. But it did not work – in the fleeting moments when he emerged from his torpor he found nothing had changed. He could not blot out the horror of Hudson's death, or erase his crippling sense of guilt.

'There something you want to tell me?' she asked.

'There isn't anything. Just leave me alone.'

Caleb felt the bed relieved of her weight and heard her tut-tutting sadly as she left the room. He was both glad and sorry she had gone, and the contradiction typified his plight. It was, he realised, an impossible situation, but he could not bring himself to act. Tormented by a nagging fear that somewhere outside the drawn curtains things were happening – events that were disastrous to him – he could still not summon up the energy or discipline to go out and *do* something, although he was fully aware he was destroying himself by loafing in the four-walled seclusion of his room. He desperately *wanted* something to *happen* to snap him out of his lethargy. And his only hope, he was convinced, was a visit from the police. Then he would know what they knew, and be in a position to convince them of his innocence, or at least satisfy them that it had all been a ghastly mistake.

The impending crack-up had been further precipitated by his inability to find Ben and talk things over. For at one point he had felt certain he could wriggle out of trouble if he and Ben got their heads together, and worked out a cast iron alibi, backed with pat answers to any questions the police might put. But all attempts to find his idol had failed. Ben seemed to be deliberately avoiding him.

In a moment of wishful thinking he had thought the police might admit failure, and gradually drop their enquiries, but this he realised was a pathetically forlorn hope: the newspapers and radio kept intimating that the police were very optimistic about the outcome.

Before the inability to act had set in, he had done what he could to remove any evidence linking him with the crime: the broken fox tail had been replaced, and he had ordered a new glass for the shattered lamp. It was unfortunate that none of the dealers he had called upon had had one in stock. But he had been promised that a replacement would be available within a day or two.

For a while, he had felt cockily safe. Then the doubts had flooded in to erode his short-lived confidence. Now every footstep sounded like the tread of a policeman's boots.

Caleb added another cigarette stub to the mounting pile in the ashtray, lit a fresh one and waited.

Superintendent Porter ordered the police car to stop at the

end of the road. If the lad was as violent as he had been led to believe, he did not want to alert him. From his experience he knew that Caleb could well be glued to a window waiting for the police to call, and he did not want to give him the opportunity of skipping out the back way or, and it was a possibility he could not afford to ignore, grabbing hold of a gun and attempting to shoot his way out. As a precaution, he had detailed another plain-clothes man to accompany him, Sergeant Rowan and Wilcox. They had all been told to carry truncheons.

'From what I hear, he's a big lad with a disposition to cut up rough at the drop of a hat. So be careful.'

Minutes earlier the car, which carried no identifying marks, had cruised slowly past the house to enable Porter to decide on a plan for entering, without affording Caleb too much time in which to act. After a brief consultation, it had been agreed that it would be best to approach the house from opposite ends of the street. Porter would walk up the front steps and hammer on the door, while Rowan and the others would slip down the area steps and position themselves on either side of the door to Caleb's flat.

'I'll go first,' said Porter, heaving himself out of the rear door. 'It'll take me five minutes to go around the block. When you see me turn the corner, start walking. O.K?'

The three men nodded. 'And don't forget. If he shows the least sign of any trouble, clobber him good and proper. I'll do the explaining afterwards. I'm not having anyone hurt for a bastard like him.'

Rowan turned to the other two officers: 'Hit him hard – if you have to – and don't worry, they've got heads like cobble stones,' and he immediately regretted it, for it gave a glimpse of the prejudice he tried so hard to suppress.

They watched Porter walk slowly away, then turn, and for some unknown reason give them a broad wink.

Rowan said, 'He's not as bloody cheerful as he makes out. Can't say I blame him. He's the one who takes the can back if any of us get hurt.'

When they saw Porter turn the corner a few minutes later, they eased out of the car and walked slowly – a discreet few feet between them – towards the house. There was no tell-tale movement of a curtain as they approached, and to their immense relief no shattering explosions.

As they came abreast of the area gate, they slipped quietly down the steps and positioned themselves on either side of the door, and listened to Porter's shoes crunching up the front steps. They waited anxiously for his knock. Suddenly Rowan noticed the rug-covered scooter. A finger tip to his lips requested silence, as he gently lifted a corner of the rug. When he saw the shattered lamp he gave a thumbs up sign and nodded his head.

Although they were expecting it, the knock caught them by surprise. It was so loud and emphatic. Minutes seemed to pass before a woman's voice said, 'What you want?'

Porter said, 'I am a police officer. Are you Mrs Jones?'

They heard no reply, but assumed she had nodded assent, for Porter went on, 'May I come in? I'd like to talk to your son.'

The woman said, 'Oh, my dear Jesus.'

Rowan tried the door-handle, felt it turn, then threw himself into the flat shouting, 'Don't move anybody. This is the police.'

He felt a trifle foolish when he realised he was shouting to an empty kitchen. Ahead was another door which he gingerly opened and peered through. On the opposite side of the room, framed by a door, stood a coloured youth whose eyes communicated total fear.

Rowan moved towards him. Behind him came the other two officers. He shouted, quite unnecessarily, 'Don't do anything damned stupid, son. We're all armed.'

The coloured boy fell into an armchair and began sobbing convulsively.

'Christ,' thought Rowan. 'What an anti-climax. So this is the dreaded tearaway. They're all the bloody same when the cards are down. Wind and piss.'

'All right, George?'

Rowan turned and saw Porter entering the room with a deeply distressed coloured woman who he realised must be Caleb's mother.

'No trouble at all, sir. Don't think there will be either.'

Porter's voice roughened. 'Right, son. Stand up and let's see your face. Kind of surprised to see us, eh?'

'No. I've been expecting you.' The voice came from a head buried in a cushion at the back of the chair.

'All right, Sergeant. Get him up.'

Rowan and the other officers moved to the chair and yanked Caleb to his feet, their hands moving briskly and efficiently over his clothing.

'He's clean, sir,' said Rowan, feeling ashamed that this weeping boy had instilled such a sense of fear.

The woman pushed her way forward and confronted Porter. 'What you want with him? I'm his mother. Anything you need to know, you ask *me*.'

Porter said as kindly as he could, 'I'd be obliged if you kept out of this for a moment. Let the lad speak for himself. He's big enough.'

The woman sat down in a chair, her eyes glinting angrily, her hands fidgeting nervously with the piping on the arms.

Porter fixed Caleb with a nerve-breaking stare, and remained silent for a full minute. Caleb shifted his eyes away until Porter barked, 'Look at me, lad. Don't turn away. Now tell me, why were you expecting us?'

'I don't know,' whispered Caleb.

'You don't know, eh. Now that seems an odd admission. Can't be many lads of your age who sit at home expecting the police to call.'

'I just was, that's all.'

His mother interrupted. 'You speak up, Wykeham. If you got nothing to hide, you tell the man.'

Rowan snapped, 'How come you've broken the lamp on your scooter?'

'I had an accident,' mumbled Caleb.

'That's pretty obvious. They don't break of their own accord. I want to know when, where and *how*.'

Porter said sternly, 'There's a lot of other things that need explaining. Like a missing page from a phone book.'

Caleb looked at the four grim-faced men and began to shake uncontrollably. They had come as he wished, but it wasn't quite the same as he had visualised. They seemed to know everything. And he realised to his own distress that guilt was etched on every line of his face.

His mother broke in, hesitant, but determined to protect him. 'If you got something to explain you being here, you tell me. Otherwise, how can he help?'

Porter said, 'I am investigating the murder of a man, and I have reason to believe that Caleb can help me.'

'Caleb! Who's that Caleb!'

'I'm sorry, that's the name he's known by.'

'Not in this home. His name's Wykeham.'

'Sorry. Wykeham. He's only got to convince us that he knows nothing about it and we'll leave you and him in peace. But I still want to know – and insist on knowing – why he was expecting us. You're his mother. You've only got to look at him to know there's something on his mind.'

'He won't talk to me,' she said miserably. 'The boy is sick of something.' Her voice took on a note of stern rebuke.

130

'Wykeham, you tell these gentlemen everything they ask. Otherwise I wash my hands of you.'

Caleb mumbled, 'Not here.' His voice was almost inaudible as he appealed to Porter, 'Can we go somewhere else?'

'You heard that, Mrs Jones. He's not been ordered to come with us. He's asked to come of his own free will.'

'I think it better for all if he did.'

Porter said, 'I must ask permission for one of my officers to search your son's room. It may mean taking some articles away. Have I your permission? I will give you a receipt for anything that is removed.'

The taciturn nod of her head gave them approval.

Rowan said, 'We shall also need to take away the scooter outside.' Again her head jogged.

An officer went into the bedroom with Caleb while he collected his cigarettes and a jacket.

Porter poked his head in and said, 'Right then! Ready?'

Caleb nodded, and Porter spotted the furtive movement of his hand as something was dropped by the bed and kicked underneath.

'I'll have that, whatever it is, laddie,' he said, bending to retrieve a crushed ball of paper. When he smoothed it out he saw it was the missing page from the telephone directory. The arm he put across Caleb's shoulder was almost avuncular. 'Right. Upstairs. I'll say this for you, son. You're going out of your way not to make things too hard for us. It'll be to your advantage, don't worry.'

Two of the detectives took an arm each, not in a firm grip, but more as a gentle reminder that they were there in case he had second thoughts about going quietly.

Porter wondered why the lad hadn't had the common sense to destroy the piece of paper; he must have known how incriminating it was. But it wasn't for him to worry about. Criminals did do incredibly stupid things – thank God: otherwise they would never be caught. Caleb hadn't burned the piece of paper or flushed it away, and that, as far as he was concerned, was all that mattered.

He turned to the officer who had been detailed to search the room. 'All this clobber will have to go to the lab for blood tests. The scooter'll have to go too. So you'll need a van. And keep the old lady out. We can't risk her taking something away.'

Caleb was taken up the area steps, and told to sit in the middle of the rear seat with his arms outstretched, while Sergeant Rowan and Wilcox sat either side, pinning his arms to the upholstery with their backs.

'I won't be any trouble, sir,' protested Caleb.

'I'm sure you won't,' said Rowan. 'But don't you fret, it's a short ride and we'll be there before you have time to be uncomfortable.'

On the doorstep, Porter was telling Mrs Jones there was nothing for her to worry about; her son would be brought home as soon as he had satisfied the police he had nothing to do with the crime.

'What about a solicitor for him, sir?'

'That isn't necessary. Your son is only helping us at this stage.'

'He not under arrest then?'

'No, Mrs Jones. If at any time he is, he will be formally cautioned and charged. Then you will be informed, and can consult a solicitor – anyone you like – on Legal Aid.' He made it sound like a big favour.

By then, Porter told himself, it would be too late for even the sharpest legal brain to do much for him. Caleb looked ready to sing, and he didn't want any shyster solicitor mucking it up by advising him of his rights, which meant he was not obliged to say anything, no matter what promises or threats were made. And he couldn't think of any solicitor not adding the warning that if he had any sense he wouldn't even speak his name aloud.

Porter wanted a voluntary statement, signed, sealed and on his desk before Caleb even knew there were such things as rights. Like all policemen, he knew you could never get a conviction if you got bogged down with the rights of the individual, and thought the Judges' Rules were a detective's bible. The law if rigidly adhered to was the crooks' greatest ally.

Mrs Jones said, 'How long will you keep him, sir?'

'That rather depends on him, I'm afraid. If at any time he asks to see you, I'll do what I can to facilitate a visit; but you must bear in mind he isn't a juvenile.' He thought he ought to get that in quickly before she started creating a fuss about being kept from her son. The promise of things to come might leave him unmolested long enough to get all he wanted from Caleb. Then the two of them could weep on each other's shoulders till the cows came home.

'Thank you for your kindness, sir,' she said, and Porter, astonished, replied, 'Think nothing of it.'

As he walked down to the waiting car, he turned and saw her waving towards Caleb, then registering hurt that he did not wave back. Unaware that his arms were pinioned, she took it as a deliberate snub and totally in keeping with his recent attitude. She went back inside firmly resolved to let him stew in his own juice until he pleaded to see her.

Porter grunted as he eased into the seat alongside the driver. 'Back to the nick,' he ordered.

Caleb said, 'My mother thought I ignored her. I wanted to wave. Now she'll think I've washed my hands of her.'

Porter turned his head and snapped, 'She'd be better off shot of you, son. You're trouble with a capital T.'

The drive back was silent, with the detectives on either

133

side of Caleb playing a nerve-breaking game of keeping him in a state of total suspense by their tight-lipped, eyes ahead attitude.

Once Porter had looked over his shoulder and muttered in a matter of fact tone, 'Lad, you're on your own now and up to your neck in trouble. When we get there, you'll be advised to tell me everything, before it's too late.'

And as the car swung into the courtyard at the rear of the station, Caleb, his arms now numbed by the pressure on his biceps, asked, 'Is Ben here?'

Rowan, his professionalism picking up the anxiety signal, said, 'As the Superintendent said, you're on your Jack Jones. Ben's deserted you.'

They hustled Caleb into the C.I.D. room where he was made to empty his pockets and hand over his braces, while an inventory of the contents was laboriously written out. 'You'll get everything back if and when you leave here,' said Rowan in a voice that implied the chances were very slim indeed.

'Are you going to third degree me?' asked Caleb in the tone of a boy expecting a beating, but hoping to hear his fears are groundless.

Porter said, 'What do you think we are, lad – the Gestapo? No, I want you to have a good night's sleep, then we'll have a nice long chat in the morning, when you've had plenty of time to think things over.'

Then Rowan formally asked him if he would mind being finger-printed. 'You are within your rights to refuse, but it's in your own interest not to. It only means I'll have to apply to a magistrate, and that wastes time and makes people angry.'

Caleb agreed, anxious to show he was co-operative, and fearful of upsetting this man who terrified him. Although his voice never rose, he somehow managed to convey the impression that he could be *very, very* hard if crossed.

Rowan produced a C3/13, 'print form', inked Caleb's fingers, and recorded the impressions in the specially indexed squares.

Caleb was handed a pen and told to write his signature on the form as confirmation that they were his fingerprints.

After being allowed to wash his hands, he was taken down to a cell by the jailer, who locked him in without uttering a word. The cell was windowless and white-tiled, with one low wattage bulb, well out of reach, burning on a short flex. A hard palliase lay on the scrubbed boards that served as a bed, and there was a toilet at the end. It was flushed from outside in case an occupant tried to destroy any evidence. A small shuttered grille was in the centre of the door, and to the right was a bell button with a notice saying if he needed assitance at any time he should ring. There was also a small Judas hole to the left of the grille through which the jailer could keep observation without being seen.

The heavy door clanged shut, and he heard the key turning in two locks. Caleb felt as if he were alone in a stranded lift. He went to the grille, but found it could not be opened from inside. It was essential, he told himself, to concentrate on his plight as calmly as possible; so he stretched out on the hard bed, but he could not think about anything except the discomfort. He rose, removed his boots, and lay down again, only to find he wanted to urinate. A notice above the toilet said: Leave this as you would wish to find it.

The words sent a chill of fright through him, and he wondered what would happen to him if he soiled the seat: would someone come in and beat him insensible? He returned to the bed without having relieved himself, and lay staring at the yellow bulb, and wondering if Ben was in an adjoining cell. Hours seemed to pass and no one came near

135

him, and even when he pressed an ear to the door he could not hear anything – not even the murmur of voices. The bell button seemed to act like a magnet, and he found his eyes continually returning to it. He experienced a compelling urge to get up and press it. Instead of the gentle ring of a door-bell, it set off a clanging like a burglar alarm. It rang for several seconds before the grille slid back and an angry voice demanded, 'What do you want now?'

Caleb's mouth was so dry he could barely get the words out. 'I want to talk to the Inspector who brought me in.'

'Don't let him hear you call him Inspector, son. He'll have your guts for garters. He's a Superintendent. Anyway, he told me you're not to be disturbed.'

Caleb said, 'I must see him.'

'I'll have a word with him. But it's no guarantee he'll come down.'

The grille closed, and Caleb went back to the bed and waited for what seemed an eternity before the grate of keys and the tumbling of locks was heard, and the door opened and Porter walked in.

Porter looking menacingly huge, said sternly, 'Now what is it, laddie? I'm a busy man. I've got lots of work to do. I can't have you wasting my time.'

'How long are you keeping me in here? You said you wanted to talk to me. Not leave me alone.'

'Like I told you. I want you to have a good rest first. There's plenty of time. Now me, if I were in your shoes, I wouldn't want to rush things.'

Caleb asked, 'Have you arrested Ben too?'

'Let's get this straight. No one has been arrested. As for your mate Ben, I'm afraid I can't discuss that. I can tell you this little tit-bit thought. He's helping us. By God, he's helping us. Got his head screwed on the right way, has Ben.'

136

Caleb, who was clutching the waistband of his trousers to keep them from falling down, said incredulously, 'Ben would never talk. He's not like that.'

Porter inclined his head, 'Life's full of surprises, lad. Those we think of as our best friends are often the first to let us down.' He glanced around the bare cell and said, 'Got everything you need?' and without waiting for a reply added, 'Good. Now get your head down.'

'What time is it then? I can't sleep.'

'It's later than you think. But just to show we're not being unhelpful I'll ask you one question. The clothes you've got on. They the ones you were wearing on the night?'

Caleb shook his head. 'No sir.' The answer was out before he realised it. He seemed to be saying things against his better judgement.

Porter said, 'Not that it matters. We'll have to have a look at what you're wearing anyhow. I'm off now. Have a good think about things. Oh, there's one other thing. A doctor will come to take a sample of your blood. He'll need your permission. I assume you'll give it.'

Caleb nodded helplessly. First the fingerprinting, now the blood sample. Although he didn't have to agree, everyone took it for granted that he would.

A sense of helplessness flooded through him as the door shut once more. The attitude of the police confused him. He had steeled himself to answer a barrage of questions, but they did not seem in the least interested. He wanted them to question him, so that he could find out what they knew. But they just didn't seem to care on their part. Perhaps they knew it all.

In the corridor outside, Porter said to the jailer, 'Don't answer the bell when he rings – and he will. Just peep in from time to time to see he's all right.'

Then Porter invited Sergeant Rowan to join him for a drink in the public house opposite.

The two detectives carried their drinks over to a corner table and relaxed. It was not until they were half way through them that Rowan ventured to raise the question of Caleb.

'What's the next move, sir?'

'I want our friend Caleb to sweat it out for a while. He's ready to talk now, but it would probably be a load of old cobblers he trotted out – still hoping to get out from under. When he talks I want him to cough the lot.'

'What about this mate Ben he keeps rabbitting on about?' asked Rowan.

'That's it. Ben's obviously the key to all this, and our friend Caleb is dying to see his mate before he opens up. At the moment he thinks he's inside and talking. Well, he will be soon. Then I think we'll play them off against each other.'

Rowan said, 'We'll play Mr Hardy and Mr Soft?'

'Something like that, George. We'll just have to see how things go.'

Caleb had rung the bell repeatedly but no one had come to see him. He slumped down on the bed and covered his eyes with his handkerchief, but nothing would shut out the light which seemed to grow brighter with the passing of time, while the cell seemed to be getting smaller and more airless.

Chapter XXI

Picking up Ben had not been the simple task that Porter had anticipated, for when he and the same three officers called at the garage where he worked, a rather bored foreman had mumbled that he was around the place somewhere. His tone implied that he didn't really care where he was, just so long as he kept out of his way. But when two grease-boys, who had been detailed to fetch him, returned and said they could not find him anywhere, the foreman grew angry and led them to the clocking-on machine. Drawing Ben's buff-coloured card from the rack, he exploded, 'The little shyster has clocked on as you can see, then buggered off. Mark my words, he'll slip back in and act as if nothing has happened. Then expect the boss to pay him for a full day.'

Porter was not in the least interested in the firm being defrauded; he was solely concerned with the prospect that Ben might have skipped, and brusquely told the foreman to get Ben's home address.

'If you find him, tell him he needn't bother coming back – except to collect his cards. And that's a fact,' said the foreman.

When Mrs Clegg opened the door, she heard who Porter was without any marked dismay, and said Little Ben was at work, or should be. Porter experienced a sinking feeling. It seemed that an arduous, time-consuming search lay ahead.

'He's not at his work. We've just called there,' he said patiently.

'Well search me. Where is he then? He went off as usual.'

'Took no extra money or clothing?'

'Not that I know of. Mind *you*, he never tells me a thing,' she said cheerfully. 'Since he lost his scooter he's been like a bear with a sore head.'

'Maybe we can help him find it – that is, if you'll tell us where he is.'

Mrs Clegg looked reprovingly at Porter. 'I've just *told* you, he's at *work*. If he isn't . . .' She left the sentence unfinished. 'Anyway, what do you want him for? He's not in trouble, is he?'

'No. It's just that he might be able to help us with some information.'

'Oh, well that's good. I'm sure he will if he can.'

Porter was surprised when she didn't request any more information, and merely shrugged when he said he would have to insist on looking round the flat.

'Go on. Don't believe me. Have a look under the bed. He's not a bad boy . . . just football mad . . . morning, noon and night,' she said by way of explanation.

Porter briefly scanned the flat, went into Ben's bedroom and took in the accumulated evidence of a football fan. Once again he went through the formal explanation that he would have to remove certain articles from the room.

Bewildered, Mrs Clegg said, 'I *do* wish his father was here. He would know so much better than me what to do. Ben don't like anyone, not even me, tampering with his stuff. It's as much as he'll do to let me clean the room.'

Porter was aware that there was a note of pride in her voice which belied the critical words. She was like so many mothers he had encountered who had no-good children – love blinded them to the flaws. It amazed him that she had not yet asked him the purpose of his visit.

On the way out, Porter again pressed her as to the possible whereabouts of her son.

'Honestly, I can't think of anywhere; unless he's with that girl of his. Though that's not likely. She works too. Sweet little thing. Steadying influence she'll be on him. And about time too, even if I say so myself.'

Fortunately, she knew her name and address.

Back in the car, he said to Rowan, 'What do you think?'

The sergeant replied, 'Might just as well turn her place over. Otherwise it will mean staking out the garage, and his mother's place. Maybe they've nipped round there for a bit of nooky.'

'At this time of day!' said Porter, but even so he instructed the driver to go to Jeannie's address.

A name-tag on a bell confirmed they had the right number, and fortunately for them another resident had conveniently left the front door propped open with half a brick. They tip-toed up the linoed stairs until they came to the numbered door they were seeking. Porter rapped the knocker and waited, but getting no response, knelt and lifted the letter-box and peered through.

Straightening, he brushed his knees although they had not touched the floor, and said, 'Someone's in. The toilet's just been flushed. Wake them up, George.'

Rowan drew his truncheon and hit the door so hard that he split a panel. 'Open up, we know you're there. It's the police.'

A young girl's voice shrilled angrily, 'Knock it off, you'll have the bloody door down.'

Porter, in his most authoritative voice threatened, 'We will if you don't unlock it.'

A bolt clicked, and the door opened a foot to reveal Jeannie's head. 'Who are you?'

Rowan gave the door a hefty push with the flat of his

hand and sent her stumbling back into the room. As they went in she stood scowling, and hugging a man's flannel dressing-gown around her. She reminded Porter of a wild kitten, with her close-cropped hair and black shadowed eyes.

'All right, where's your boy friend?'

'What boy friend?' she said insolently. 'You've got no bloody right barging in like this.'

An even more aggressively insolent voice drew the policeman's attention to the toilet door. 'You got a search warrant?'

Ben stood in his Y-front pants, propping himself against an upright, disdaining any attempt to cover himself. 'Let's see the warrant,' he said, moving towards them with an outstretched hand. 'Come on, don't be shy.'

Porter motioned for Wilcox to close the door. 'A warrant isn't necessary – the young lady invited us in.'

'You lying bugger,' squealed Jeannie. 'Your bully boy nearly knocked me flat.'

Porter said sternly, 'Cut out the lip – the pair of you. Otherwise I'll be looking into the girl's age and what you've been up to.'

Ben looked at him with intense loathing, and said with affected weariness, 'Cut out the horse-shit. She's passed the age of consent. Just tell me the reason for busting in like a load of gangsters.'

Porter said, 'I want you down the road for questioning.'

'About?'

'Defrauding your firm. Now get some clothes on. You might appeal to this little slut like that, but you just make me feel like throwing up.'

Ben bent low, hands on hips, and emitted a bellow of forced laughter. 'Come off it. I haven't defrauded anyone. What's the con?'

142

Porter said, 'You clocked on, but didn't inform your employer you were leaving.'

Jeannie broke in. 'You don't arrest someone for pinching an hour of the boss's time. Christ, you'd have half the country inside if you did.'

'It'll do as an excuse,' snapped Porter. 'When we get there, maybe we'll have a chat about something more serious – like murder for instance.'

Ben clenched his fists and said aggressively, 'You must be out of your teeny-weeny mind. Murder! What do I know about murder? Anyway, I want to contact a solicitor. Until I do I'm not moving or saying a thing.'

Rowan and Wilcox moved threateningly towards Ben, who to their surprise stood his ground. Rowan put his hand on his shoulder and was impressed at the strength of the shrug that threw his hand off. He would not like to meet the big bastard alone down a dark alley. He found himself saying appeasingly, 'Come on, Ben. No point in getting angry. It's better to go the easy way. Come on, put some clothes on.'

Ben gave a shrug that indicated he thought they were all quite mad, and turned into the bedroom, his bare shoulders conveying utter contempt.

Porter, who was thinking to himself that a nasty incident had been averted, was brought back to the room by a sharp and vicious rap on his ankle. The next minute he found himself grabbing Jeannie's two wrists in one hand, and holding her at arm's length as she hacked away at his shins. The dressing-gown flew open, and he saw that she had nothing on beneath. But he was too occupied with keeping her at a distance to worry about her nudity. She may not have had any shoes on, but she still managed to hurt, and he was surprised at the supple strength of the young girl.

'Look, if you know what's good for you, lass, you'll keep

out of this. Take a tip from me, go sit on the bed till it's all over.'

Porter was angry with himself for finding it such a job holding the girl in check, and realised how out of condition he was.

But there was no stopping her. She screamed, and spat at him, 'You're not taking him anywhere.'

Porter motioned to Wilcox, who moved swiftly forward and pinioned Jeannie from the back.

'O.K. have it your own way. You can come along and keep him company,' said Porter. Jeannie writhed and twisted, but she was no match for the young officer.

'Take your dirty bloody mitts off me. If I'm coming with you, at least let me get some clothes,' she spat.

Porter lighted a cigarette and said, 'Not unless you promise to behave. Otherwise, you can come as you are. We're no prudes down the road. What's good enough for Ben, is good enough for us.'

Jeannie indicated she would be no further trouble, and the officer followed her into the bedroom and turned his back while she changed.

Ben, meanwhile, had got his clothes on. 'Right. I'm ready. But you can take it from me – all you'll get is my name and address. I want a solicitor.'

After the routine formalities at the police station, they were escorted into separate cells. Ben repeatedly demanded a solicitor, and actually produced the name of one. Porter airily told him he could not be contacted on the telephone, although he was perfectly aware that Ben knew he had not even made the effort to call him.

Ben, unawed and belligerent, said, 'That's all right with me then. Until I get one, I'm not saying a dickie bird.'

Porter said, 'I'll give you a little time to think about it.

144

Meanwhile, we'll chat up your friend Caleb. See if he's more co-operative.'

All Ben said was, 'He's no friend of mine – so don't go insulting people.'

Porter called Rowan into his office, and after a few minutes conversation decided Caleb was the weak link and they should, therefore, concentrate on him. Rowan would go in first and play the tough officer with a streak of cruelty as wide as a motorway. Then Porter would go in and adopt the role of a kindly, more understanding man who just wanted to help a lad in trouble.

Enough time had elapsed for the forensic laboratories to provide them with a preliminary report of what had been found during examinations, and tests on Caleb's clothing, boots, scooter, covering rug and fox tail. They decided to see what effect the news would have on the coloured boy.

When Rowan went into the cell Caleb, who had been lying on his bed, jumped to his feet and protested loudly, 'I've been ringing that bell for hours.'

'Sorry, no one heard it. It gets stuck from time to time.'

Caleb flounced petulantly on to the bed, but Rowan brought him to his feet immediately, 'Right! On your feet. This is no doss house, so stop lolling around.'

The tension mounted as Rowan took an overlong time in selecting a cigarette, lighting it, examining the tip, then sitting on the bed, leaving Caleb standing while he thumbed his way through a note-book.

Finally he grunted, put the book away and said with a note of finality, 'Well, Caleb, or Jones, or Wykeham. What have you got to say for yourself, eh?'

Caleb said plaintively, 'Can I have one of your cigarettes? I've finished all mine.'

'Sorry. No smoking allowed in here.' The note-book

145

emerged again. There was another long and studied silence. Rowan looked up and said with a smile, 'Things don't look too good for you, son. How's this for a start? There's a lot of blood on your clothing that is the same group as the dead man's. They didn't even have to look for it. No sir, they could scrape it off.'

Caleb was silenced by a wave of Rowan's hand. 'Hold your horses. That's only the tip of the iceberg.' He flipped over two pages. 'A comparison microscope shows that fibres found on the rug match up in all respects to fibres from the fox tail remnant which we found near the spot where you murdered Hudson.'

Again Caleb was silenced. 'Don't be in too much of a hurry, Caleb. I've only begun. The new tail you bought is completely different. If that strikes you as being a bit technical, I'll spell it out. It means there are two of them. The one you had on the scooter when you killed him, and the other you bought later to throw us off the scent. A check round the shops will expose that little ruse. Now this bit will kill you – we've also got evidence that proves you busted your lamp while putting the boot in.'

Caleb was stunned and silent, trying desperately to force his brain to think lucidly, and make him say *something* that would minimise the mounting pile of incriminating evidence.

'Think about it, Caleb. There's enough there to put you away for life. I'll have to tell your mother and father all about it now, won't I? I should think they'll be really disappointed in you.'

Caleb said, 'I can't face them after this. What's Ben say? I'm not saying anything till I know.' He lowered his head and said weakly, 'He told me I mustn't.'

Rowan pursed his lips. 'Well, that's just too bad – for you I mean. I can't tell you what Ben says. After all, he's perfectly entitled to defend himself. And I must say he's doing that with a vengeance. Boy, are you up the creek without a paddle!'

Rowan studied the youth with dispassionate eyes, and realised he would soon snap under the pressure. There would be no need for any physical force, and this pleased him greatly, for he was basically opposed to violence. Violence, he felt, brought him down to their level, which wasn't a particularly flattering thought.

'You are a squalid disgrace to your family, Caleb, and no mistake. The best thing you can do is make a clean breast of things and get it over with. Unless of course you have an explanation for all the things I've mentioned? If you have, I'm a ready listener.'

Caleb slumped down on the bed, and this time he was allowed to remain seated.

'I can't say a thing till I know what Ben wants,' he pleaded. 'Tell me what he says first.'

Rowan rose and signalled for the jailer to open the door. 'I'll see you later. When you're in a better frame of mind to help. And I don't want you flopping around on the bed. You need to be wide awake to appreciate the trouble you are in. So stay on your feet.'

Porter and Rowan saw Ben together, and within a few minutes knew they were right – Caleb was going to be the weak link. Ben was surly, unco-operative and completely unintimidated by his surroundings. He ignored their warnings not to smoke, and underlined his defiance by dropping the stub on the floor, grinding it out with his boot, and lighting a fresh one. 'Until I've been charged, you've no right to have me in a cell, let alone telling me not to smoke. If you don't like it – let me out.'

Porter ignored him and said, 'I've checked with the

147

station officer near your home and find you reported your scooter missing. Now it strikes me as a remarkable coincidence that it should have happened the night Hudson was murdered?'

'Who?'

'Hudson, the referee. The man whose death we think you can help us with.'

'I can't help at all.'

'Or won't?' queried Rowan.

'When you allow me to have a solicitor present I'll answer anything. Till then . . .' and he shook his head vigorously.

They spent half an hour in the cell badgering and bullying him, and getting nowhere. Rowan even struck him twice – two hard blows, one in the stomach and another near the kidneys where they could not be seen – but although Ben had winced with the pain, he had remained stubbornly silent, content to let his eyes express contempt.

Porter was far from discouraged, knowing it often took time to get a person to talk. He remained convinced that the truth would come from Caleb.

They returned to his office, where a woman sergeant told them she had got nowhere with Jeannie.

'They've obviously got their heads together over this, sir. Every time I asked her anything she referred me to her boy friend. When I got around to the night Hudson was killed, she just said she was too busy helping Ben look for his scooter.'

Porter sighed and put on his overcoat. 'We'll go over for a drink and let it rest, for a while. Time's on our side. Jesus, they haven't even had time to get numb bums yet.'

In the public house, some newspapermen were waiting patiently for information, and Porter went over and told them they were at liberty to say two youths were helping them with their enquiries. No names were available and he couldn't give them any further information. 'Christ, we've only had time to check their personal belongings.'

'We understand there's a girl in there with them,' asked one reporter.

'That's true, but leave her out of it for the moment. We don't even know if she had any part in it.'

'Will there be any charges later?'

'Not for quite a while. We've only had rough and ready reports from the lab and we've still got a long, long way to go. That, I'm afraid gentlemen, is all I can give you.'

The reporters thanked him and went out to find telephones and put over the copy that would virtually signal the end of the story until someone was charged.

When Porter and Rowan returned to the police station, the jailer complained that the cell bells had not stopped ringing. Ben and Jeannie had simply wanted to protest at being kept locked up and deprived of their liberty, and the services of a solicitor. In accordance with his orders, he had left Caleb's ring unanswered.

'He's doing his nut, that one, pacing up and down, and whining like a sick dog. When he's not doing that he's on his knees – praying to Allah, I suppose. If it gets too hard on his knees I'll get him a prayer mat.'

Porter said, 'I'm calling it a day. We'll have another go in the morning. The lab might have something on Ben by then.'

He paused at the door and said testily, 'By the way, Caleb's a Catholic, so don't knock the prayers. His fear of God might loosen his tongue more than his fear of us.'

Before Porter *could* call it a day, however, the intercom on his desk buzzed noisily. When he answered, the station sergeant said, 'The girl's father's down here playing merry hell. Wants to see the officer in charge.'

'I'll be right down,' barked Porter.

The call was not unexpected. Porter had been anticipating it ever since he had left instructions for a constable to call round to explain Jeannie's absence. He had already decided on the attitude he would adopt: brusque to the point of rudeness, aggressively intimidating and patently annoyed that anyone should have the temerity to call and interrupt him in the middle of a major investigation.

Porter strode into the main office, slammed the door hard and took an instant dislike to a small dapperly dressed man, pacing angrily up and down, punching a clenched fist into the palm of his hand. Porter recognised the signs of a little man anxious to convey the impression that he meant business. It impressed him as much as a puppy barking.

Porter stood menacingly in front of him, and said with all the authority he could muster. 'I am Chief Superintendent Porter. What do you want?'

The little man brushed a hand over the patent-leather hair. 'I am Mr Basil Carter ...' pausing when it evoked no response, and adding, 'Jeannie's father. I demand an explanation.'

'Do you now?' said Porter. 'Well, you can try asking for one, but nobody demands anything in here. Get that. And let's get it clear – even if you ask me nicely I might still not give it.'

The man wilted, and his voice took on a whining aggrieved note as he moved the hand from his hair and wiped it across a perfectly dry brow. 'I'm sorry. Forgive me. I'm a bit distraught.'

'That's better. Now, if you'll come with me we may be able to help.'

Porter turned briskly on his heels and walked out, leaving Jeannie's father to scurry after him.

Inside his office, Porter placed a solid-seat chair in front of his desk and gestured for Mr Carter to sit down.

'Right. Let's hear what's on your mind. But keep it brief. I've had a long, long day.'

Jeannie's father tried to sound angry, but his indignation petered out into a feeble protest. Lowering his head, and tugging at the inch of white shirt cuff he said, 'It's not on. I mean, it's not right for a father to be told by a police constable that his daughter's been carted off to the station like a common felon. Damn it, there are more tactful ways of doing it than sending someone round for all the neighbours to see and gloat over. What kind of picture will they have of me?'

Porter said sarcastically, 'Mr Carter, I had considered writing you a personal note, but I thought you might not appreciate the delay entailed.'

'There's no need to address me like that. I'm entitled to an explanation.'

Porter's fist thudded down on the desk top so hard that the ash tray and telephone bounced. 'You're not entitled to a bloody thing. I'm the one who's entitled to an explanation, but your hard little bitch of a daughter won't give me one.'

'Superintendent! She is my only daughter. I'm a widower myself. It's to be expected that I should be deeply upset,' he said, dabbing at his eyes with a breast pocket handkerchief that had been so long in his pocket that the creases were discoloured. 'I've dedicated myself to bringing Jeannie up as a credit to the memory of her dear mother.'

'She's a slut,' said Porter disdainfully. 'Your sweet little Jeannie swears like a fish wife, and has the morals of an alley cat.'

Mr Carter rose to his feet, his face grey with indignation. 'How dare you say that!'

Porter barely disguised his contempt. 'When we called

round your daughter had just had intercourse in *your* bed. She had nothing on but *your* dressing-gown. And her bed-mate was a big bastard who we have every reason to believe kicked a man to death.'

Mr Carter buried his shining head in his hands and began to cry. He whispered, 'I can't believe it. Jeannie wouldn't do a thing like that. In her mother's bed, you say! That's unmentionably obscene.'

'A bit lacking in respect too,' said Porter sourly.

Carter pounded his forehead in an absurdly dramatic manner, and then asked, 'Tell me, sir. What exactly were they doing?'

'Look,' said Porter patiently. 'I didn't play the role of voyeur.'

Carter stood up and paced across the office. 'You could be wrong. I mean, you didn't catch them at it – red-handed.'

Porter said, 'Look, Mr Carter. I'm involved in a murder investigation, not a sex probe.'

Mr Carter said, 'I suppose I should be thinking of hiring a solicitor?'

Porter told him, 'At this stage there's no point, she's merely helping us.'

Porter walked him to the staircase. 'Just keep going – you'll find your way out.'

The visit had served a useful purpose – all the parents involved now knew they could expect cold comfort if they pestered the police.

Chapter XXII

The news from the forensic laboratories was depressing. Rushed, but none the less thorough tests had produced nothing that could possibly lead to a prosecution against Ben. Several minute stains on a pair of jeans and a shirt had responded to various blood tests, but the reaction was so weak and the amount so small that the scientist was unable to say how old it was, what group it belonged to, or even whether it was human. And the boots were so spotless that the scientific officer had no doubts at all that they had been thoroughly scoured and then coated with polish. He also expressed the view that the clothing had recently been to the dry-cleaners.

'Proof that someone sends his clobber to the cleaners is hardly evidence of murder, I'm afraid,' a disconsolate Porter had muttered over the telephone.

The scientific officer, sensing his disappointment, had promised to persist with further tests. 'There are enough of them, but frankly I'm pessimistic. Contrary to public opinion you *can* remove blood if you put your mind to it.'

Porter thanked him and appreciated his integrity. He didn't want any kindly disposed scientist giving him flimsy evidence that could be knocked for six by a defence expert.

Then purely as a precaution, he detailed Wilcox to return to the girl's home and collect her clothing for tests. 'I should have done that in the first place,' he chided himself.

Conscientiously, but without much hope of success, he asked the uniformed branch to assist in trying to find Ben's missing scooter. 'If it was nicked as he claims, then that's him in the clear. If it wasn't, then it's probably at the bottom of a gravel pit somewhere. Still, we must go through the motions.'

Having got those two niggling problems out of the way, he summoned Rowan to his office to discuss the day's tactics.

Rowan, surly and ruffled at the lack of progress, plonked into a chair and said, 'I popped downstairs to chat up the jailer. Ben is still as hard as a navy biscuit. The girl's not shifting either. They've obviously got their heads together over this. Our friend Caleb played merry hell all night. I don't know – maybe the time is ripe to have another crack at him.'

Porter remained silent, his forehead furrowed with concentration. When he emerged from his reverie, he stood up and banged the desk top. 'I've had an idea. Let's get Mrs Hudson and the two train lads down straight away. The one who was beaten up, and his pal who saw it. We'll let them have a good accidental look at our charming little trio while they're exercising. If we get a positive identification it will help us tighten the screws a bit. Not to mention the help it'll be if we ever get around to seeing the D.P.P. Linking up the football ground rumpus with the train shindig and the murder, will at least show a pattern of events.'

It took over an hour to pick up Mrs Hudson, and twice as long to collect Michael and John.

Michael's face still showed signs of the savage beating he had received on the train; dark glasses hid his bruised eyes, and a wide strip of plaster covered the bridge of his nose.

Porter took them into his office and said politely, 'I'm sorry to drag you down here, but there are one or two things I would like to check in the statements you made earlier.'

It was a feeble but good enough excuse, he thought, and solemnly went through the statements word by word, repeatedly apologising that if it seemed a little time-wasting they must appreciate it was essential that an innocent person should not suffer through some lack of attention to a minor detail. The expression on their faces clearly indicated that his scruples were not shared.

It all took less than half an hour, and when Porter glanced at his watch he realised the time was near when Ben, Jeannie and Caleb would be shepherded into the car park at the rear of the station for routine exercises.

'We'll go out the back way if you don't mind. Far more convenient for you all. You can get straight into the cars and be off.'

An iron fire escape zig-zagged its way down the back of the station, and as Porter led them out he saw the three suspects, kept a careful ten yards apart, being escorted slowly round the yard. He made certain that Mrs Hudson and the two men were alongside him on the platform before saying, 'Hold on. Must exercise a little caution here.'

He said no more, but his gaze willed them to look down. Mrs Hudson was the first to react. 'That big coloured boy,' she whispered. 'That's him. The one after the match. I'd recognise him anywhere.'

Michael said triumphantly, 'I recognise all three. The big one was responsible for beating me up. The girl, and the coloured chap were with him.'

John said, 'I recognise the one who attacked Michael, and the coloured bloke and girl.'

Porter convincingly expressed surprise. 'Really! Well that's a turn up for the book. You absolutely certain?'

The three people assured him that they had no doubts whatsoever, and were prepared to swear to it upon oath.

Porter sighed, 'There's a little more to it than that, I'm afraid. To be really acceptable evidence it would have to be done at a formal identity parade. Now, if you're willing to

155

attend one, I could arrange it very quickly.' He deliberately introduced a note of doubt into his voice. But it was unnecessary. They all agreed with alacrity.

As he ushered them back into his office, pointing out that the encounter was unfortunate in one way but most opportune in another, he arranged for them all to return to the station after they had had a meal at the police's expense.

'It isn't according to the rules, and I'm afraid that we are expected to work very much by the book. Therefore, I'd appreciate it if you didn't mention this casual encounter to anyone. You never know, some bright lawyer might suggest it was a put-up job.'

Rounding up the necessary and suitable people for three identity parades took much longer than normal, for it was essential that those lined up with Caleb should be coloured. But once enough people had been assembled, the parades went off without a hitch.

Ben was the first to be identified. Michael, who had been told to go slowly up and down the line and if he recognised anyone to stop, and place a hand on his shoulder, walked unnecessarily along the line twice before tapping Ben on the collar bone. The line was then switched around before John was brought out. He unhesitatingly picked out Ben.

The same thing happened when Jeannie was paraded with a group of girls who had been recruited from a nearby garment factory. Finally, when Caleb was lined up, he was so agitated and self-incriminating, that he gave the impression he had something to hide. Separately, John and Michael promptly identified him, although it was hardly necessary for them to place a hand on him. Guilt was engraved on his face and he recoiled when they approached him.

The parade was kept intact for Mrs Hudson, who walked briskly up the line and stopped directly opposite Caleb, but she refrained from touching him. Instead she stepped back and pointed, saying, 'That is the one.'

When they had returned to their cells, and Mrs Hudson and the two men seen off the premises, Porter held another conference with Rowan.

Obviously elated, he said, 'That will go a long way with a jury. It establishes all three were together at the same time.'

Rowan, less exuberant, said, 'It doesn't link our friend Ben with the killing. It only proves that he and the bird were involved in the punch-up on the train.'

'Maybe. But it's progress, George. Pieces in the jig-saw. Now let's pop down and see if we've managed to ruffle Ben's calm.'

The reaction was not what they had hoped for. Ben remained completely unruffled, insisting that the two men were mistaken or had been put up to it. Beyond that he would not go. 'I'm still waiting for a solicitor,' he said arrogantly. 'I'm not saying a thing till then, not even if you kick the living daylights out of me, and I'm sure you'll be getting around to that pretty soon.'

They fared no better when they went in to see Jeannie, who repeated like a gramophone record, 'I can only repeat what Ben told you. So there.'

'Well, just you tell us what he said,' invited Porter.

'That would only be repeating what you know already,' she said insolently.

They bullied her for twenty minutes, but she refused to add anything. It was obvious to the two detectives that she was adhering to a carefully pre-arranged plan.

Porter decided to see Caleb on his own. The coloured boy looked guilty, and quickly got off the bunk and stood rigidly to attention when Porter entered the cell. 'Sit down, laddie,' he said. 'I shouldn't be sticking my neck out like

157

this, but I want to help you. I can't do that, however, unless you are prepared to help yourself.'

In contrast to the bullying manner adopted by Rowan earlier, he went out of his way to appear sympathetic and kindly. He handed a packet of cigarettes to Caleb, who eagerly took one and gulped the smoke down so quickly that it set him off coughing. Porter patted his back until he got his breath back, then told him to keep the packet.

'I suppose you know who those people were who picked you out at the identity parade?'

Caleb dumbly nodded his head in affirmation.

Porter paced up and down like a man with a problem on his mind. 'Surely you must see it's in your own interests to help me all you can. Ben has told us everything. He's a hard case, that one – let you sink as long as he can remain afloat. He's the bright boy all right.'

Caleb shook his head miserably, as if trying to convey that he acknowledged his own stupidity.

'You wanted to help Ben, didn't you?' Again the head nodded. 'And quite rightly you wouldn't say anything until Ben did?'

Caleb buried his head in his hands and sobbed. 'Ben said we would all be safe so long as we didn't talk.'

'In that case, I'm afraid he's dropped you in it, laddie. Take a tip from me, don't carry the can alone. Tell me everything. Leave nothing out. Look – you can do it two ways. Write it down yourself, or I'll get someone to take it down for you. Then you can sign it. That's fair, surely?'

Caleb sat silent, carefully thinking about the proposition, before blurting that he would prefer someone else to write it down for him.

Porter felt a glow of triumph, but concealed it as Caleb was taken from the cell into the charge room, where Rowan took out several statement forms, tapped them level and

158

laid them in a neat pile on top of the desk.

Tea was brought in from the canteen, and Caleb was given the most comfortable seat.

Porter said, as if it were of no great significance, 'There's a mere formality that I must go through.' Whereupon he formally cautioned Caleb that he was not obliged to say anything unless he wished to do so, but that everything he did say would be taken down and might be used in evidence.

Caleb said, 'I understand,' and Rowan meticulously wrote the reply in a note-book. Caleb was unaware that he had been formally cautioned.

Then slowly and deliberately, the coloured boy recounted the events that had led up to the death of Hudson. Porter halted him from time to time to extract a vital piece of evidence, such as how the visit to Hudson's house was first discussed, how they traced the address, how they rode there, and how and why the Belisha beacon was smashed. When Caleb began to race ahead, he was slowed down and warned to think carefully. His memory was jogged when there was any danger of his omitting the slightest detail.

'We don't want to leave *anything* out,' said Porter.

Caleb broke down completely when he came to describe Hudson's death. He was allowed a short break and a cigarette before being urged to continue. Rowan took the opportunity to flex his cramp-stiff fingers.

Patiently and skilfully Porter encouraged him to explain why Hudson had been killed. Hard-bitten as he was, he found it difficult to conceal his horror that it had been done simply because Hudson had awarded a penalty.

'You did it just for that!' he said with astonishment.

'Ben did. Not me. I didn't really care one way or the other who won.'

'Your own motive was different?'

159

'I didn't want to hurt him, but I didn't want to be kicked out for being chicken. You've never been coloured, sir, so you wouldn't understand.'

Fervently, Caleb went on to describe his great fear that he would be cold-shouldered by the gang. The long rambling explanation was punctuated with tearful pleadings that he hadn't really intended anyone to be hurt.

Porter irritably signalled to Rowan to stop writing. He didn't want the statement bogged under by such an improbable excuse. Although the police were not expected to produce a motive for a murder, it went a long, long way with a jury if they could. For the man-in-the-street juror liked to know *why* before reaching a verdict.

Porter was aware that killing a man because he gave a wrong decision would make sense to them, whereas the ramblings of Caleb would appear nonsense. And if they were included in the statement they might give the impression that Caleb was a bit mental.

It took Rowan three hours to complete the statement – which was in effect a full confession – read it through, correct it, get Caleb to initial the alterations, and finally sign it.

In his own hand, Caleb wrote that the statement was made of his own free will, and he had been allowed to make what alterations he wished, and that the statement was true.

Porter stood up, stretched his arms above his head and yawned. He felt tired and surprised at the lack of achievement he felt. It had all been a bit too easy. Rowan, on the other hand, could not conceal his delight, slapping Caleb on the back and telling him he had done the smartest thing, and that a jury always went out of its way to help the repentant.

When Caleb was formally charged with the murder of Hudson, he nodded and looked relieved.

160

'Now go along and have a good night's sleep, laddie. Or would you like to see your parents?'

Caleb said, 'No thank you, sir. I'd prefer to do that in the morning if I could.'

'Certainly you can. After a good breakfast,' said Porter.

The coloured boy said, 'If it isn't too much trouble, I would like to see a priest, too.'

'I'll lay one on. Anything else?' asked Porter.

Caleb shook his head. 'I'm surprised Ben let me down. Tell him that.'

'I will, laddie. I will,' said the Superintendent.

When he was returned to his cell, three blankets and a pillow were taken in. His head had barely touched the pillow before he was asleep.

Porter told Rowan to nip off home, and to arrange for transport to collect the boy's parents in the morning. 'Oh, and lay on a priest, will you, George?'

Rowan slipped into his overcoat and gave a wide grin. 'After that little lot he can have a Cardinal. Goodnight, sir.'

Porter sat at his desk and told himself that there was still a long, long way to go yet. Caleb was safely in the landing net, but Ben, the big fish, was still likely to slip the hook. So far, he was clear on the murder charge, for no jury would take Caleb's uncorroborated statement as evidence of Ben's guilt. And any fair-minded judge would go out of his way to pin-point the dangers of such a statement.

Porter cat-napped in his office until 2 a.m. before waking Ben in his cell, and casually tossing him Caleb's statement to read. He hoped Ben would rise to the fresh bait, for he had carefully chosen the time when his resistance would be at its lowest. Porter stood silent, hands on hips, in a get-yourself-out-of-that pose, calculating that the admission

161

spoke more eloquently than anything he could say.

Ben swung his feet on to the floor, wiped his eyes and was immediately wide awake. He read carefully through the statement before throwing it disdainfully at Porter's feet. 'Surely you didn't wake me at this bloody hour to read that load of old toffee?'

'Is that what you call it? I suggest you take another look. You'll see Caleb's signed it before making it, and he signed it again afterwards. Quite voluntarily,' murmured Porter.

Ben spat, 'Who are you kidding? Signed it, you mean, after you and your bouncer pal had knocked seven bells of shit out of him.'

'No one laid a finger on him. There was no need.'

Ben stretched his arms above his head and gave an exaggeratedly false yawn to express his disbelief. 'Tell it to the marines. Anyway, what's all that guff got to do with me? I think the nigger made it up. *He* did it all right, and now he's trying to row in an innocent party to keep him company. I wouldn't mind betting you put him up to it.'

Porter was astonished at the way the youth refused to be intimidated. Although he had no criminal record he seemed to be well acquainted with the tactics adopted by the professional crook when in custody: refuse to say a word that might incriminate, and leave it to the police to find the necessary evidence to support a charge. Never forgetting that more convictions are obtained through verbal indiscretions than mountains of evidence. He had obviously impressed this upon the girl, too.

Porter took another tack in an attempt to shatter his confidence.

'Tests have revealed the presence of blood stains on your clothing that are not yours. Anything to say to that?' He hoped the lie would catch him unguarded.

'Nope.'

162

'It's very serious.'

Ben's bored voice indicated that he was finding the superintendent rather tedious. 'Look, if you've found some blood, then use it as evidence. But don't bowl in here thinking I'm going to drop myself in the cart because you're up a gum tree. Do your own dirty work.'

Porter pressed on, but the big youth refused to confirm any of Caleb's allegations, or for that matter offer an explanation. He simply dismissed it as, 'a lot of spiteful cobblers'.

Porter persisted, however, with a steady barrage of questions. When he stopped, Ben gave a sarcastic round of applause and said, 'Finished?'

'No. I've still got a few more.'

'Look,' said Ben, his anger mounting, 'I want to get back to kip. I'm not going to agree to something I didn't do just to make you happy. I'll go without my beauty sleep if necessary. *I* won't get so tired that I'll say *anything*, just for a bit of peace. Caleb made it all up. If you want to charge me with murder, go ahead. If not, let me go. Because according to the law, you can't hold me any longer without a charge.'

Porter paced up and down the cell, head down, hands behind his back, hoping the silence might have an unnerving effect on Ben, but when he glanced up he saw that the youth wasn't even looking at him. His hands were across the back of his head and his eyes were closed.

Porter snapped at him, brusque and threatening. 'You don't deny you were on the train when it was wrecked and a man was seriously injured? A man who has identified you as his assailant.'

Ben's eyes remained closed and his reply had a cultivated weariness. 'That's where you are so wrong. I do deny it. And if you've got your little book handy you can write this

163

down: I didn't kill anyone and I didn't fill anybody in.'

Whereupon he turned over to indicate that the interview was over, and he was going to sleep. Porter was tempted to yank him upright and strike him, but restrained himself, realising that he needed to retain the image of considerate fairness he had so assiduously cultivated. Momentarily, he regretted letting Rowan go home, for while not expecting a confession from Ben, he had not anticipated such a blase reaction. He felt sure that a few hairline cracks would have appeared in the wall of brashness with which Ben surrounded himself. If Rowan had been around he would have let him, and a couple of beefy detective constables, have half an hour alone in the locked cell with him. The thought was not a pandering to brutality just for the sake of it, but a carefully reasoned piece of logic. For ironically, hard cases often talked after a beating. They would show their bruises in the remand prison, and proudly claim that they had not said a word until they had been battered into submission. The existence of injuries being sufficient proof to other criminals whose respect they valued, that they had not succumbed until the very last minute.

Porter rang for the jailer, realising he would get nothing from Ben. But he was seriously worried about keeping him in custody any longer without a charge. Again, the silly rules which made the hunting and apprehension of criminals a kind of sporting game had intruded.

Back in his office he sat smoking and thinking about the quandary he was in. The obvious answer, he realised, was a holding charge. It meant charging a person for a minor, even trivial offence, in order to keep him in custody until a major charge could be brought.

Porter gave instructions for Ben to be brought up to the charge room. There in the presence of the station officer he formally charged him with causing grievous bodily harm to

164

a person on a train.

Asked if he wished to say anything in answer to the charge, Ben replied, 'I deny it. And I want it recorded that I asked for a lawyer.'

Porter moved his hand as if brushing away an irritating midge and snapped, 'Lock him up.'

By the time he got back to his office, it was nearly four a.m. Despite the lateness of the hour and his own dog-tiredness, he decided it might pay dividends to visit Jeannie.

The interview was a complete waste of time. When he showed her Caleb's statement she merely shrugged and said, 'If you want to take the word of a coloured, then go ahead. I know nothing about it. Neither does Ben. We keep telling you that.'

Porter had her taken up to the charge room where she was formally charged with assaulting a police officer – namely himself – in the execution of his duty. Jeannie, completely unperturbed, said, 'What a carve up! When did I assault a big ugly bugger like you?'

'When I called at your home.'

She sneered. 'You must be hard up for an excuse to keep me here. That's all I can say.'

'I am,' he said. 'But don't worry, we'll think up something better later on. I can, of course, charge you with causing a breach of the peace on a train. It's as broad as it's long.'

He walked home slowly, feeling he needed the exercise and the fresh air, while he racked his brain for some means to crack Ben and the girl. But he realised he was stuck. Caleb was as neatly trussed as an oven-ready turkey. The most reluctant-to-convict jury would have no hesitation in finding him guilty on the evidence. But all there was against the other two was an uncorroborated statement.

By the time he had slipped into bed, he had made up his mind to go to the Director of Public Prosecutions Department and present the evidence so far assembled. He would ask if there was sufficient evidence to justify a charge of murder being brought against Ben.

Chapter XXIII

Sergeant Rowan sat sipping his pint of beer in the crowded, smokey saloon bar of a public house near Buckingham Palace. He sat hunched and glowering, to ensure that the seat opposite remained untaken. Several customers had tentatively put a claiming hand on the back-rest, then turned away, preferring to stand rather than suffer the company of a man who looked so belligerent.

The beer tasted awful to Rowan, and he felt the first twinges of heartburn near his sternum, which he knew was brought on by nervous tension. For his mind was really with Superintendent Porter who was with an official of the Director of Public Prosecutions Department in nearby Buckingham Gate, seeking legal guidance whether or not they had enough evidence to go ahead with a murder charge against Ben and Jeannie.

It was the awareness of the cold, dispassionate appraisal that was going on in the detached-from-life atmosphere of the D.P.P.'s Department that depressed Rowan. There, cocooned from reality, legal experts adjudicated with Olympian aloofness on how good a job the copper on the beat had done. He crossed his fingers and hoped Porter was winning.

For the D.P.P.'s Department was no respecter of persons – least of all policemen – and the go-ahead was only given when it was felt certain a conviction could be obtained. Seldom was a police officer told he had all the evidence necessary; mostly, he was told where the gaps were, and sent off to 'tighten up the loose nuts'. On rarer occasions, he was told he did not stand a cat-in-hell's chance of securing a conviction, and no further action was recommended. This, all policemen dreaded, for it was tantamount to failure in the eyes of their superiors.

All these thoughts were running through Rowan's mind. Porter was a good copper who would not be overawed by the fire-irons and fender atmosphere of the Department where murder was an abstract thing; but no matter what he said, the last word would be with the Director's Department.

Suddenly he heard the sound of a military band and was grateful for the distraction. Gulping down his drink, he walked out into the street in time to see a uniformed constable with white gloves holding up the traffic by Queen Victoria's statue, in order to make way for the band of the Grenadier Guards, which headed a column of guardsmen marching briskly with rifles at the slope and bayonets fixed. They had just left Chelsea Barracks for the daily ritual of changing the guard at the Palace.

Rowan felt his steps quicken to keep time with the beat of the big drum, and he hurried along the pavement.

There was a flash of silver from the sword of an officer, and the shrill barks of commands being given, followed immediately by the thud and crunch of boots, polished to a black glass finish, as they hit the pink-coloured parade ground.

Nearly two hours had elapsed since Porter had entered the building. He had been ushered to a comfortable chair while

167

a senior member of the Director's staff had read through all the evidence after being given a resume of the case.

He was a tall, scholarly looking man, who wore the traditional lawyer's uniform of black jacket and pin-striped trousers, stiff winged collar and dark grey tie. From time to time he rattled his teeth with the end of a gold-plated pen.

He signalled that he had finished by pushing the pile of documents away from him across the desk, and looking at Porter over the top of his half-moon spectacles. 'Well, Superintendent, what do you think?'

'I think we've got a pretty good case, sir.'

'You think that, do you, Superintendent? That's interesting.'

For some unaccountable reason, Porter felt himself thrown on the defensive. 'The statement of the coloured youth is pretty damning.'

The official gave what Porter could only describe as an old-fashioned look. 'A trifle pat, isn't it? I notice, too, that it was taken down by one of your officers.'

'Meaning, sir?'

The spectacles were removed and wagged as if to emphasise the point. 'Meaning it would have carried more weight if it had been in the accused's own hand.'

Porter said as sharply as he dared, 'He made the statement quite voluntarily. If his memory needed jogging we jogged it, that's all. What's down there he signed for, sir.'

The official rose and walked round his desk, offered Porter a cigarette and patted him on the shoulder. 'Now, now. Let's not get rattled. Important as the statement is, confessions have been known to be withdrawn or ruled inadmissible. If that happened here, you wouldn't have much of a case left.'

Porter reminded him of the forensic evidence and the identity parade.

168

'True, Mr Porter. But you know forensic evidence doesn't cut a lot of ice with juries. Bit above their heads. They like good independent witnesses.' He touched the tips of his fingers delicately together. 'And I'm afraid your witnesses aren't witnesses to the murder. Not by a long chalk.'

Porter began to remonstrate, but was cut short. 'Superintendent, I know what this means to you. Hours of nonstop work. You think I'm being unnecessarily pessimistic. I'm not. Let's forget the coloured boy for a minute and concentrate on the other two. The girl you can forget. You've nothing against her except the holding charge. Proceed with that by all means.' He wagged the gold-plated pen. 'Murder, no. And that's not too bad a thing. A girl can have the effect of introducing a sympathetic element. And as for Caleb's statement, that is not admissible evidence against her or the boy friend. That's not an opinion – that's law.'

The official became benign and ordered coffee as if to signify the discussion was over, although Porter knew that more dispiriting news was to come.

'Superintendent, I ought to warn you. I say this reluctantly, but nevertheless I must say it. In a perfect society, every man's word is accepted at its face value. But here, despite our seemingly enlightened attitudes, juries have an unshakable belief that coloured folk are less reliable than our own people when questions of truthfulness are involved.

They talked for another twenty minutes, during which time the legal adviser emphasised the strong points of the police case and underlined its weaknesses.

Porter shook hands, gathered his coat, and left to break the news to Rowan.

The ceremony ended and Rowan walked slowly back towards the public house. His eye caught Porter standing on the far pavement waiting for a gap in the traffic in order to cross. He looked dejected, with his head buried deep into his paisley scarf. The weight of his bulky black brief case dragged down his shoulder.

Rowan waited by the kerb, and when Porter stepped beside him, asked, 'How did it go, sir?'

Porter shook his head, and gave a thumbs down signal. 'Bloody awful.'

Inside the bar, Porter looked around for a quiet table.

He said irritably, 'Well, George, he wasn't too pleased with our work. We can forget the girl completely, and as far as Ben is concerned he doesn't think we have a leg to stand on unless we get some additional evidence. What's more, he was none too happy about Caleb.'

Rowan said pointedly, 'It seems to me that he doesn't think we've got much of a case. That's what it amounts to, isn't it?'

'Oh, we've got a case all right, George, It's just that it isn't watertight. He suggested it could be if we got Ben and Jeannie to testify against Caleb.'

'A deal,' said Rowan disgustedly.

'Well, he didn't exactly put it that way. He'd have us both sued for slander if he heard that. But you are right – that's what it adds up to. In order to nail young Caleb we've got to let Ben and his little bint off the hook.'

Rowan remained silent for quite a while. 'That's a shabby trick,' he finally said. 'I think Caleb's story is the right one.'

Porter patted him gently on the shoulder. 'George, you astonish me. Of course it's true. But the gentleman I've just left doesn't see things quite the same way as we do. He's solely concerned with a successful prosecution. We're too near the game, George. I'll bet you a pound to a pinch he's

170

forgotten it already.'

They caught a taxi to the railway station, and Porter sat silent in his seat peering out of the window but seeing nothing. Rowan was wise enough not to disturb him.

As the taxi neared the station, Porter sighed and said, 'Well, George, we ballsed it up, and no mistake. I should have let you and a couple of the lads have Ben boy alone for a little while. Now it's too late. He's comfortably tucked up in a remand prison where we can't get at him. And knowing our Ben, he'll have fixed up a solicitor too by now.'

Back in the office, Porter and Rowan spent an hour sifting through the evidence and wondering how they could add to the evidence against Ben.

One slim chance remained. Porter ordered an intensification of the search for Ben's missing scooter.

Chapter XXIV

Police Constable Raymond Jenkins cursed aloud as the rain ran down the collar of his regulation issue raincoat and trickled down his neck, soaking his shirt. The bottoms of his trousers were already sodden where the rain had run off the hem of his coat. He glanced at his watch and was encouraged to see that he only had another fifteen minutes to go before his shift ended. By God, he told himself, I earn my corn the hard way. Without a doubt, the soaking would bring on his fibrositis. He felt full of self-pity.

For three days now he had been detached from his normal duties and instructed, with a score of other beat-pounders, to comb the division for a missing motor scooter. He had tackled the job with great diligence – something that he doubted his colleagues had done. Conscientiously he had examined coal cellars, derelict houses, lock-up garages, vacant plots, scrap metal yards and car dumps. But he had found nothing. Seek and ye shall find, had been his attitude when he started. Now he felt dejected, uncomfortable and thoroughly convinced that the scooter wasn't on his patch. He would have liked to find it. Apart from being a feather in his cap, his unflagging efforts deserved rewarding. But he would have to accept disappointment, for he had almost covered the area which had been allocated to him. And he wasn't sorry. It couldn't have been a worse day for searching. The rain had fallen incessantly, straight down like steel rods, and so hard that the roads and pavements had been covered with bouncing gouts of water. What's more, he thought glancing up at the grey sky, there's still plenty more left up there.

Ahead of him lay a filthy canal, the surface of which was so lashed by rain spots that he couldn't detect any flow in the water. Anyway, frogmen had searched the stretch and found nothing. Beyond it through the rain haze he could see what had once been allotments and the outline of an old tool shed. Jenkins walked slowly towards it, then halted. Although a great believer in leaving no stone unturned, the line had to be drawn somewhere. He had searched far more likely spots than the shed and found nothing. But apart from anything, it seemed inconceivable that the boy whose scooter they were seeking would have been half-baked enough to put it somewhere so close to where he lived. If he had stuck it in the shed it would have been found long before now.

Preoccupied with his thoughts, Jenkins didn't look where he was putting his feet, and stepped on a particularly soggy piece of ground. He felt the mud and water squelch through the lace holes of his boots. Angrily, he retraced his steps

172

and headed for the police station.

He hoped one of his colleagues had had better luck and found the bloody scooter. Judging from the briefing they had got, it was very important. Well, he could assure his inspector that it wasn't on the section he had been detailed to search. It had been a dull, monotonous chore, but he had done it with painstaking thoroughness. That's what they pay me for, he told himself, with more than a hint of pomposity.

Chapter XXV

A four-deep queue straggled along the pavement, hugging the soot-grimed wall by the public entrance to the Old Bailey. It had begun to form at 2 a.m., when a duffle-coated man arrived with a sleeping bag, folding stool, camping stove, saucepan and tin of tomato soup, and propped himself against the solid oak door. By 9.30 a.m. it snaked round the corner.

A constable in the distinctive uniform of the City of London Police had been despatched from nearby Snow Hill Station to keep the queue, which threatened to obstruct the footpath, in good humoured order. To save many of them from a pointless wait he had started at the tail of the queue and moved three quarters of the way up, warning them that as accommodation was so limited in the public gallery, there was no hope of the majority getting in. But he was ignored. They preferred to wait, stoically stamping on the ground to keep the blood circulating, and blowing hot breath on dead fingers. They confirmed the constable's long held theory that the British loved forming queues.

Porter saw the tail-end of the queue, and was amazed that people could wait patiently for hours just to see a person fighting for survival.

When he walked into the main hall, he saw many of the witnesses who would be called. He spotted Jeannie beside her martyr father. She was hardly recognisable in a neat woollen dress of respectable length, buckled shoes with medium-height heels and a hair style that would not have looked out of place in a bank. It was a deceiving picture, but who was he to argue? Someone had obviously spoken to her about the image she should make in court. The cropped hair, jeans and boots would definitely have undermined her testimony.

Jeannie was the most fortunate of the trio. She had appeared in a magistrates court and been fined twenty-five pounds for assaulting a police officer.

It made Porter feel like throwing up when she waved to him across the hall.

Ben was on bail after being committed for trial on the charge of causing grievous bodily harm. He, too, would be called to give evidence against Caleb.

Porter walked into the court and saw the exhibits officer busy preparing the exhibits. Caleb's scooter rested against the front of the desk.

The famous court looked most unforbidding. The huge Sword of Justice above the Lord Mayor's seat looked like a theatrical prop, and the glass-sided dock held no fears.

Porter dumped his brief case on the table, and booked himself a seat – the one he would occupy throughout the hearing. Then he went down to the basement cafeteria for a cup of tea. On the way he passed Mrs Hudson, and stopped just long enough to ask her how she was, and to assure her there was nothing to worry about.

Rowan was sitting drinking tea.

174

'Morning, George. All fit for the fray?'

'Yes, sir. I can't see anything upsetting the apple cart.'

'No. It's pretty cut and dried. Not quite the way I would have liked it, but there we are.'

They hurried back to the court to wait for the pageantry and paraphernalia which marked the opening of a new session. Porter found it all a little too detached from reality for his liking.

Suddenly, the buzz of subdued conversation was halted by three sharp knocks on the door of the judge's dais. Everyone rose, and a black-robed usher bellowed like a fair-ground barker:

'All persons who have anything to do before My Lords the Queen's Justices of Oyer and Terminer and General Goal Delivery for the jurisdiction of the Central Criminal Court draw near and give your attendance.'

Mr Justice Howitt, in his ermine trimmed scarlet robe, black tippet and wide black belt, nodded to the court and the various officials, who bowed back in turn.

When everyone was seated, the Clerk of the Court, who was sitting below the judge, gave his wig a tug and said, 'Put up the prisoner.'

There was a sound of a cell door clanging below the dock, followed by the scuffle of feet on stone steps. Then Caleb appeared between two uniformed prison officers who propelled him to the front of the dock, where he stood knees-twitching, licking his lips and gripping the wooden sill in front of him so hard that his knuckles showed grey through the black skin. The charge was read to him.

'How say you Wykeham Jefferson Jones, are you guilty or not guilty?'

Caleb seemed to be having trouble getting the reply out. He swallowed deeply several times, and the crowded court wondered whether something really dramatic was about to

175

occur, such as a plea of guilty. But Caleb made a final swallow and said in a low voice, 'Not guilty.'

Mr Horace Judkins, Queen's Counsel, stood up and assumed an actor's pose – left hand on his hip and right elbow resting on the bench in front of him, with his hand cupping his chin. He was a tall, heavy-shouldered man with a mane of dark curly hair, tufts of which sprouted out from the sides of his grey wig.

He was a hard man to oppose. He marshalled his facts thoroughly, and was like a terrier when it came to cross-examination, and he never asked a question to which he did not know the answer.

In a voice as smooth as his gown, he began to open the prosecution's case. Painstakingly, Mr Judkins drew a heart-tugging picture of life in the Hudson home, implanting in the jury's mind the image of a devoted family suddenly shattered by a tragic loss. When he had finished, he had no doubt whatsoever that the jury's sympathies were with the widow.

He then referred to the match and the violence outside the ground. 'That was the beginning of a flash trail that led to the brutal murder of Hudson. His widow will describe the horror of that night when their car was waylaid. She will also tell you that she recognised one man that night. On man hell bent on trouble.'

Mr Judkins swung round, tugged his gown, and pointed an accusing finger at Caleb. 'She will tell you that he was the man. The one who now stands accused of murder.'

Mr Judkins went on, remorselessly piling up the evidence against Caleb. The scene on the train, the telephone directory, the scooter and finally Caleb's confession.

He sipped gently at a glass of water, deliberately creating an atmosphere of tension before dealing with the statement.

'In that statement signed, and acknowledged as the truth,

176

in his own hand, Jones will tell you how this hideous crime came to be planned, then ruthlessly executed. It reveals that this was no on the spur-of-the-moment fit of anger. But a coldly calculated, pre-conceived killing. No words of mine can describe the horror on that common when poor Hudson was done to death. But the words of the accused can. He has put it all down in this statement.' Mr Judkins tapped the statement with his forefinger and shook his head. 'Yes, this statement.'

Caleb gave a low moan and buried his face in his hands. Every head turned towards the dock, and scores of eyes took in the picture of Caleb sobbing and banging the wooden rest in front of him with his forehead.

Mr Judkins was annoyed at being interrupted in full flow, but realised it was to his advantage. No jury could possibly witness such a scene without believing it implied guilt.

Caleb was given a glass of water, and told by one of the prison officers, in a voice that could not be heard beyond the dock, to pull himself together because he wasn't doing himself much good in the eyes of the jury by such carryings on.

When Mr Judkins reached the scientific evidence, the timbre of his voice hardened, and he leaned towards the jury, emphasising each point with a rap of his pen on his portable document stand. Experience had taught him that when it came to outlining details of vital evidence that tended to be above the jurors' heads, it was essential to introduce some dramatics to impress its importance upon them.

Porter thought he was doing a magnificent job. He just wondered what tack he would take when it came to the evidence of Jeannie and Ben.

Mr Judkins cleared his throat and intoned. 'Now we

177

come to a part of the prosecution's case which I shall be the first to admit should be treated with great circumspection – great circumspection.' He deliberately repeated the word as he wished the jury to be confused.

'In the prisoner's statement, he introduces the names of two people who he claims were involved in the murder. Irrespective of what *he* claims, the law of this land – and quite rightly too – says emphatically, that allegations made by an accused cannot be used as evidence against a third party. I do not need to tell you, nay, warn you, why that stipulation is made. An aggrieved person knowing the game is up may feel like implicating someone else for no other reason than malice. In our humble submission, that it the case here.'

Mr Judkins went through his gown tugging, wig-tipping routine. 'Separate and independent evidence must be laid against the two people Jones attempts to incriminate. It is not my task to adjudge reasons for his actions. But I am entitled to say that after exhaustive police enquiries no charge of murder has been laid against them. In fact, they are being called to give evidence for the prosecution. I say no more. Just ponder on that.'

He paused. 'I must, of course, add this. We do not rely on their evidence, important as it is. There is other evidence of a far more damning nature. Evidence that will convince you, beyond all reasonable doubt, that Jones – and Jones alone – murdered Hudson.'

When he glanced at his watch he felt with a glow of pride that his timing had been perfect. It left just five minutes to the lunch adjournment.

He concluded: 'With the assistance of my learned friends, I will call that evidence before you.'

When the court resumed after lunch, the remaining time

178

until the court rose was taken up with plans and photographs of the murder scene being submitted and approved, and the pathologist's evidence.

Cross-examined by Mr Gilbert Hare, Q.C., for the defence, the pathologist said he was quite unable to say whether the injuries were inflicted by more than one person.

'They were all consistent with a brutal attack and could have been inflicted by a pair of heavy boots, a solid piece of machinery – even fists.'

And there the first day of the hearing ended.

Chapter XXVI

Day Two: Most of the day was taken up with the evidence of Mrs Hudson, who spoke loudly and clearly of the football match, and the scene when the car was almost overturned. She was adamant in her recollections.

There was *no doubt* in her mind that the accused was one of the people taking part in the attack.

Under heavy cross-examination, she remained insistent that she had seen Jones outside the ground. No, she was not *mistaken* when she picked him out at the identity parade. Mr Hare did not question her too harshly or over-long. For two reasons: she had the sympathy of the jury, who would not take too kindly to a grieving widow being grilled; and her evidence in no way connected the accused with the actual murder.

It was all rather dull and formal.

The two men, Michael and John, were then called to give evidence. Both identified Caleb as having been on the train, although both stressed he had done nothing violent.

179

'In fairness to the accused,' Mr Judkins asked Michael, 'Did you subsequently identify another man as the person who attacked you?'

'Yes.'

Mr Hare decided to make a legal submission. In the absence of the jury, Mr Hare propounded that it was quite wrong that Clegg should be allowed to give evidence while still awaiting trial. It would, he submitted, have been far better for all if Clegg had been dealt with first.

'Should he have been found guilty, it is of obvious advantage to the defence. If not, the prosecution gains,' he said. He cited precedents and read extracts from numerous other cases.

Mr Justice Howitt said that Clegg's evidence should be heard. After all, he could be discredited under cross-examination.

'The jury aren't fools, Mr Hare,' he said. 'They can't be led by the nose these days.'

Day Three: The forensic evidence was heard. The defence called their own witnesses to challenge and rebut it. But when it was concluded the general opinion was that the defence had made little or no impact.

Several people dozed off in the public gallery and were awakened by angry officials.

The case came to life again when Detective Chief Superintendent Cyril Porter took the oath and gave his evidence. He gave it professionally and impartially. He seemed to have an encyclopaedic memory of the events and their proper sequence.

When it came to Caleb's statement, Mr Judkins said, 'If I read it out from a copy, will you please follow it from the original you now have in your hand?'

The gasps and murmurings indicated that the statement

180

had a telling effect both on the jury and public.

Rarely had the jury looked at the accused unless they had been directed to do so. Now they all turned their heads and stared at him. Caleb did not enhance his chances by lowering his head and averting his eyes. When Porter had completed reading it, several members of the jury exchanged knowing glances at each other. When Mr Hare rose to cross-examine, he was fully aware that the statement had had a damning effect.

'Superintendent,' he began. 'You are telling the jury that this is a statement of fact?' The question was put in a manner that implied the jury would be absolute fools to believe it.

'No, sir. I am merely saying that the accused signed it as being true,' corrected Porter.

'Let me put it this way, then. There are parts of the statement which you believe to be true, and parts which you do not believe to be true.'

Mr Judkins leaned back in his seat and smiled broadly. He hoped the jury would see it, and interpret it as a smile of sympathy for a colleague who was floundering and fighting a losing battle. Plenty of guns but no ammunition. Secretly he was deeply concerned, for he fully appreciated Mr Hare's tactics, even if the jury did not. He was hell bent on discrediting the statement.

Mr Judkins studied Porter's face very carefully and hoped he wouldn't fall into any traps.

Porter thought carefully before replying. 'I think I've told you, sir, how the statement came to be taken. The accused was asked if he wanted to write it down himself or dictate it, and . . .'

Mr Hare banged his fist on the wooden bench and snapped angrily, 'Superintendent, please answer my question. Which parts do you think are untrue?'

Porter looked up at the judge and said, 'Must I answer that, my Lord?'

'Yes. He insists on an answer. Let him have it.'

Porter said, 'I can only say I think the parts appertaining to the murder which the accused admits are true.'

Mr Hare turned away in disgust and exploded. 'I object most strenuously, my Lord. That is a most improper observation. It is comment.'

Mr Judkin chuckled inwardly and reminded himself that the cardinal sin was not to know the answer to a question before you put it.

The judge said benignly, 'Mr Hare. You insisted on putting it to him. Now you complain. However, I do think it is not for the officer to decide, but a question for the jury.' And he instructed the answer to be struck out, and ordered the jury to forget it. But the damage had been done for they *had* heard it.

Unabashed, Mr Hare said, 'It's rather detailed and most chronologically recorded. Doesn't that strike you as a trifle odd for a youth of his limited capabilities?'

Superintendent Porter said, 'He was in a very emotional state and seemed anxious to get it over quickly. Obviously I was in possession of a lot of information, and I stopped him from time to time and asked him about certain things. His replies were incorporated in the statement which Sergeant Rowan was writing down.'

Mr Hare said, 'He was obviously upset, you say?'

'Yes, sir.'

'So it's quite conceivable that he was not fully aware of what he was saying, or what Sergeant Rowan was writing down? Things could have been slipped in here and there?'

'No, sir. If you look at the statement you'll see that Jones initialled every correction. Then he read it through before signing it.'

Mr Hare made desperate efforts to discredit the officer. 'But Jones wasn't going out of his way to help you? It wasn't quite as voluntary as you make out? You suggested certain things?'

'Once he had made his mind up, he told us everything he knew.'

Mr Hare nodded his head. 'We are at least getting to the point, officer. Jones claims that the youth Clegg, and the girl Jeannie,' – he referred to his brief – 'Miss Carter, are responsible for Hudson's death. Let us make no mistake about it. That is what he claims. He says the wrong person is in the dock.'

'I know, sir. It's all in the statement.'

'You agree he claims he took a lesser – no, let me put it more strongly – a minor part in the attack.'

'He claims that, yes.'

'But you don't believe that any more than the part that implicates the boy and girl?' Mr Hare's voice did not conceal his disgust.

Porter said, 'It is not a question of what I believe, sir.'

Mr Hare said, 'The youth Clegg and the girl spent a long time in custody being questioned by you.'

'Not in custody. Helping, yes.'

'They were not charged, and now they appear as witnesses for the prosecution. Does that not strike you as odd?'

Mr Judkins rose, a note of reluctance in his voice. 'I am loath to interrupt my learned friend, but the Superintendent is not in a position to answer the questions my learned friend is putting to him. It was the Director's decision who should be charged and who should be called as witnesses. There is no sinister plot to be unearthed here.'

The judge said, 'If Mr Hare is suggesting there is, then he ought to say so.'

Mr Hare rose and said, 'I make no such suggestion, and

if I have inadvertently given that impression I withdraw it unreservedly.' That, in fact was what he had been alleging, and he only hoped the jury were reading between the lines.

Nevertheless, he went on for another hour trying to make out that the confession was rigged. But when he came to sit down he was not at all sure that he had achieved his objective.

Day Four: The usher bellowed: 'Call Benjamin Clegg.'

Ben walked with a steady step to the witness box. His appearance had altered considerably since his arrest. His hair had grown, and the stubble had been replaced by a style that now needed parting. Further, he was dressed in his one suit – a dark pin stripe with a flared waist and narrow trouser bottoms. His shoes were flashy and high-heeled, but in no way capable of inflicting serious injuries. He looked, in fact, like one of thousands of young men to be seen strolling through the streets – trendy and with-it, but by no means aggressive in appearance.

Ben took the oath in a loud voice, and under the promptings of Mr Judkins gave his name and address and occupation.

There was even a hint of remorse in his voice when he admitted he was awaiting trial for causing grievous bodily harm to a passenger on a train.

Mr Judkins said, 'Do you recognise the accused?'

Ben looked towards the dock and said, 'Yes, Caleb.'

'Caleb?'

'Yes, that's what he liked to be called. I never knew his real name till now.'

Mr Judkins continued, 'He went around with the same gang as yourself?'

Ben looked aggrieved. 'I wouldn't call it a gang, sir. There was a bunch of us who like football, and went to games together. Caleb was one, but he wasn't all that welcome. He didn't fit in.'

Mr Judkins asked a few more questions, then stiffened and said, 'Let us not beat about the bush, Clegg. Jones is accused of murder, but he alleges that you in fact were the ringleader. He has made a statement to that effect.'

Ben gave a hurt smile. 'I know. It was read out to me by Mr Porter.'

'Well! What do you say to it?'

'A load of rubbish, and Caleb knows it. He made no secret what he was going to do. He tried to rope others in but got the cold shoulder. We all thought he was potty.'

Mr Judkins pressed upon him to enlarge, and Ben did – readily.

'We had all gone to the Cup game, and Caleb got all worked up over the ref giving a penalty. He came in to the disco where me meet at night, and said he had the bloke's address and was we interested in filling him in good and proper. We – that's Jeannie and me – didn't want anything to do with it. Neither did the others.'

Mr Judkins interrupted him there. 'We can't have anything about the girl. Only what you said to the accused, or what he said to you.'

Ben said, 'Well, he asked me to go with him. I said I'd think about it, although I knew I wouldn't. I was choked at the ref, but not that angry to do him any harm. I mean, it was just another game.'

Mr Judkin was nearing the end of Ben's evidence when he asked, 'Tell the jury this. Why do you think – no, do you *know* why Jones tried to implicate you in the murder?'

Ben shook his head in bewilderment. 'I haven't the foggiest. He was narked because we were going to chuck him out of the group.'

'Why?'

185

'Well, it all began at the disco when we was arguing about violence . . .'

Mr Hare did not give Ben a chance to continue. He was on his feet objecting most strenuously.

Mr Judkins rose and said blithely, 'I will not press the matter, my Lord.'

When it came to cross-examination, Mr Hare tried his utmost to discredit Ben. But he stuck to his story: Caleb had been on his own. He had been hell-bent on revenge, but his efforts to involve others had been rejected.

Mr Hare took up Caleb's statement and began to go through it line by line. But whenever it referred to him, Ben simply said, 'That just isn't true.'

Mr Hare said, 'Even to the extent of describing how you all rode to the house on your scooters? How you waited by the tree, how you rested your scooters against a shed?'

'Well, that can't be true for a start, because I didn't have mine. It had been stolen.'

Mr Hare said, 'You mean you reported it stolen after the murder? Why leave it so late – or were you preparing an alibi?'

Ben said, 'Well, it was obvious I wasn't going to report it lost without first having a good look. Some of the lads borrow scooters just for a giggle. Me and Jeannie looked high and low for it. If you don't believe me, ask the police.'

After two hours, Mr Hare had to admit defeat.

When he finally sat down, he gave the impression that he had demolished Ben's evidence completely. He nodded with satisfaction to his colleagues, and even raised a smile.

He fared no better when Jeannie was called. She too made a perfect witness: she answered all the questions put to her; sometimes taking long pauses before replying, as if anxious not to say anything hastily and without careful consideration.

186

Her story tallied with Ben's, and no one looking at her could really believe she was capable of taking part in an assault which resulted in a man's death.

When she stepped from the witness box, she dropped the judge a neat semi-curtsy, and a dispirited Mr Hare wondered who had put her up to that.

The judge looked up at the clock and said, 'I think this is a most convenient time to adjourn.'

The court rose.

Day Five: Superintendent Porter was briefly recalled by the defence and questioned about the missing scooter.

He said it had been reported missing, and the insurance company notified. A massive police search had been organised, but no trace of the machine had been found.

Mr Hare stood up and pronounced: 'I will now call the accused, Wykeham Jefferson Jones.' From the start, he was a hopelessly unconvincing witness. Instead of following his counsel's instructions and striding purposely, head high, to the witness box like a youth only too eager for the opportunity to clear his name, he shambled, eyes-down, seeking support from anything that conveniently came to hand.

As the usher handed him the testament, his hand shook uncontrollably, and his voice quavered and sank to an inaudible whisper when he was asked to read aloud the oath.

He stuck steadfastly to his statement, but impressed no one. Ben had been the instigator, and he had only gone along because Ben had threatened to throw him out of the gang for being chicken. But he had not done a thing to Mr Hudson except aim a kick at him which he knew couldn't have killed him. Ben had done the real damage.

And it was Ben, he said, who had started the trouble at the football match. Ben had also started the trouble on the train. *He* had been the peace-maker. Ben had suggested

187

'getting' Hudson. Ben had told him to get the address.

It all sounded very unconvincing to the jury. They had seen Ben, and the girl. And they had closely observed Jones for nearly a week. They might have believed him a bit more if he hadn't tried so hard to put it all down to Ben, and make himself appear the innocent party. Caleb struck them as a nasty youth who could only reiterate, 'It was him, not me'. The two coloured members of the jury were the most outraged of the jurors. Caleb had let down the coloured community. Because of him they could all look forward to an upsurge of racial strife. Well, they would show that blood was not thicker than water.

There was a look of defeat on Mr Hare's face when he sat down.

Mr Judkins rose, and in half an hour had torn Caleb's evidence to shreds. Some of his questions were put with a sympathetic, almost apologetic tone, as if he was only too anxious for Caleb to have an explanation.

'*Your* clothing had blood on it. *Your* scooter was damaged. It was your fox tail that was found at the scene. It was *your* statement. Signed, initialled and signed again.'

'Yes, sir.'

'So irrespective of what you say Clegg and the girl did, you were there?'

'Yes, sir.'

'Looking back. It was a wicked evil thing you did?'

'Yes, sir.'

At which point Caleb began to cry. Although he had several more questions to ask, Mr Judkins decided that this was the perfect moment to sit down.

'No more questions, my Lord,' he said, not even bothering to conceal a note of triumph in his voice.

Mr Justice Howitt decided it was time to adjourn. He wished the jurors an enjoyable weekend, and intimated that he hoped the case would end on Monday.

Day Six – the final day: Mr Judkins made his closing speech for the Crown. It was short, but all the more damning for its brevity. Without leaving out any of the salient points, he managed to convey the impression that it really was a waste of the jury's time to keep hammering home the obvious.

Mr Hare's speech for the defence was eloquent and beautifully delivered, but even he felt he was making bricks without straw. The main problem, and he knew it, was that Caleb had cut such a bad figure in the dock, and thrown far too much mud for anyone to believe him.

Nevertheless, he tried hard, and after three hours he sat down saying, 'I submit to you that after a full, dispassionate consideration of the evidence, the Crown have failed to prove this case beyond all reasonable doubt. There is only one verdict for you – Not Guilty.'

Mr Justice Howitt's summing up was a dull repetition of the evidence. And although the jury gave the impression of being totally attentive, one or two were seen to shake their heads as their eye-lids threatened to close.

He closed with the words, 'If you have any doubts, the accused must have the benefit. But if you have none, let your verdict be clear and let justice be done. Will you consider your verdict?'

The jury retired and returned after the surprisingly short absence of an hour.

Their verdict: GUILTY.

It came as no surprise to the crowded court, although there was considerable mumbling, and the usher had to call, 'Order, Order,' several times.

Caleb was ordered to stand while sentence was passed. 'Jones, you have been convicted on evidence which can leave no doubt upon the minds of everyone,' said the judge. 'I have no alternative but to sentence you to imprisonment for life. In passing sentence, I would like to say this. It was a callous, horrible crime, and one in which you tried to incriminate others. If people of other races come here, they must learn to integrate and accept the standards of their adopted country. You are still a young man and have time to learn the sporting beliefs of a country that accepts defeat as graciously as victory.'

As Caleb was led away, the judge thanked the jury and exempted them from serving again for another five years.

Nan Hudson heard the verdict, but did not wait to hear the sentence. She slipped unnoticed from the court and walked slowly towards Holborn Viaduct Station, avoiding a posse of photographers who were waiting outside the court to 'snatch' a picture of the victim's widow.

Since giving her evidence, she had sat on a hard wooden bench behind the dock, intently watching Caleb throughout his ordeal.

At first, she had been consumed with a burning desire for revenge. But gradually as the trial went on, hatred had turned to apathy. She no longer really cared what happened to the pathetic youth who had cut such a sorry picture in the witness box. Further, she had begun to have misgivings about a system that had to rely on the evidence of two such worthless youngsters as Ben and the girl to obtain a conviction. She felt tainted by being a part of it.

She had decided that whatever happened, nothing would bring Barry back and she was determined to put the past behind and start a new life with the children, away from sympathy and the stares of the curious. The first step would be to put the house up for sale. There was no hope of forgetting, surrounded by memories.

She reached the station and bought a romantic novel at a book kiosk, found an empty carriage and began the painful process of forgetting.

Porter and Rowan strolled over to 'The Magpie and Stump' opposite, to meet the Press and give them any information they might require for what are called 'background stories'.

The Pressmen, who showered drinks and congratulations on the two policemen, couldn't understand why neither of them was happy with the result.

Jeannie sat in the back row of the public seats in Court Number Four, waiting for Ben to appear.

When he did, no evidence was called, for his counsel pleaded guilty on his behalf and made a long speech in mitigation.

Ben was fined fifty pounds and given six months' suspended sentence, and warned not to let his enthusiasm for his team get the better of him, no matter how much he was provoked.

Ben was not surprised. He had been told this was the likely outcome.

Mr Carter stood on the pavement outside the Old Bailey waiting for Jeannie to join him. He was rather annoyed that none of the photographers had thought fit to take his picture. Although he had not given evidence, his daughter had played a vital part in the conviction of the coloured man. And, of course, he had a good story himself to tell of the problems confronting a widower with a young and pretty daughter to bring up.

He did not see Ben and Jeannie leave by another door, and the building was locked and bolted before he would accept that she had deliberately avoided him.

Mr Judkins and Mr Hare took a taxi cab to a public house well away from the court to have a drink together.

Mr Hare complimented Mr Judkins on the brilliant way he had handled the prosecution. Mr Judkins sympathised with Mr Hare, and said it had been tough for him as he never really had anything to go on.

'I must confess,' said Mr Hare, 'my heart wasn't in it. I abhor violence of that nature.'

He added, 'I thought old Howitt was a bit off in his remarks about people coming to this country. The boy was born here.'

Mr Judkins said, 'I agree it showed prejudice, but alas, old man, it isn't grounds for an appeal.'

Ben and Jeannie caught a bus home. Ben's parents, who had been told there was no need to attend his own trial, had a welcome-home tea waiting. Ben, however, decided on first going to the derelict allotment shed.

The scooter was still there, but he could get no response from the engine when he tried the kick-starter. Green mould covered much of the chrome and the rubber parts had perished.

'You know, Ben, you'd be better off dumping it in the canal. The insurance must pay up *now*. Anyway, it's getting a bit ropy,' said Jeannie.

Together they wheeled it to the bank, and laughed and jumped with delight as it splashed out of sight.

Ben decided to leave the home-comings till later. Hand in hand they walked to the Rovers ground and looked at the forthcoming fixtures.

'Roll on Saturday,' said Ben. 'At home to Fulham. What a rave-up that'll be.'

'You've got time to get your hair cut,' said Jeannie.